COLLEEN McCULLOUGH

The Ladies of Missalonghi

HEAD
of ZEUS

First published in Great Britain in 1987 by Hutchinson
This edition first published in 2015 by Head of Zeus Ltd

9 7 5 3 1 2 4 6 8

A catalogue record for this book is available
from the British Library.

ISBN (HB) 9781784082864
ISBN (E) 9781784082154

Printed and bound in Germany
by GGP Media GmbH, Pössneck

Head of Zeus Ltd
Clerkenwell House
45-47 Clerkenwell Green
London EC1R 0HT

WWW.HEADOFZEUS.COM

The Ladies of Missalonghi

Colleen McCullough was born in
Wellington, New South Wales. She worked
in neurophysiology at Yale Medical School
for ten years, where she wrote the record-
breaking, international bestseller
The Thorn Birds.

For Mother,
who has finally attained her dream of
living in the Blue Mountains

AUTHOR'S NOTE

For the information of readers who notice that
Missalonghi is spelled with an "a" rather than the
"o" now commonly accepted as correct, in Australia
at the time this story takes place, the old-fashioned
"a" was more usual.

"CAN YOU TELL ME, Octavia, why our luck never seems to change for the better?" asked Mrs. Drusilla Wright of her sister, adding with a sigh, "We need a new roof."

Miss Octavia Hurlingford dropped her hands into her lap, shook her head dolefully and echoed the sigh. "Oh, dear! Are you sure?"

"Denys is."

Since their nephew Denys Hurlingford ran the local ironmongery and had a thriving plumbing business as well, his word was law in such matters.

"How much will a new roof cost? Must it be a whole one? Couldn't we have the worst sheets replaced?"

"There isn't one sheet of iron worth keeping, Denys says, so we're looking at about fifty pounds, I'm afraid."

A gloomy silence fell, each sister cudgelling her brain in search of a source for the necessary funds. They were sitting side by side on a horsehair-stuffed sofa whose better days were so far in the past that no one remembered them.

3

Mrs. Drusilla Wright was hemstitching pulled threads around the border of a linen cloth with microscopically fine, meticulous skill, and Miss Octavia Hurlingford was occupied with a crochet hook, the work dangling from it as exquisitely done as the hemstitching.

"We could use the fifty pounds Father put in the bank for me when I was born," offered the third occupant of the room, anxious to make amends for the fact that she saved not a penny of her egg and butter money. She was also working, sitting on a low stool producing lace from a tatting shuttle and a ball of ecru thread, her fingers moving with the complete efficiency of a task known so well it was sightless, mindless.

"Thank you, but no," said Drusilla.

And that was the end of the only conversation occurring during the two-hour work period of Friday afternoon, for not long afterwards the hall clock began to chime four. While the last vibrations still lingered in the air, all three ladies proceeded with the automatism of long custom to put away their handicrafts, Drusilla her sewing, Octavia her crocheting, and Missy her tatting. Each lady disposed of her work inside an identical grey flannel drawstring bag, after which each lady disposed of her bag inside a battered mahogany sideboard sitting beneath the window.

The routine never, never varied. At four o'clock the two-hour handwork session in the second-best parlour came to an end, and another two-hour session began, but of a different kind. Drusilla moved to the organ which was her only treasure and only pleasure, while Octavia and Missy moved to the kitchen, there to prepare the evening meal and finish off the outside chores.

As they clustered in the doorway like three hens unsure of the pecking order, it was easy to see that Drusilla and Octavia were sisters. Each was extremely tall and each had a long, bony, anaemically fair face; but where Drusilla was sturdily large and muscular, Octavia was crabbed and diminished by a long-standing bone disease. Missy shared the height, though not so much of it, being a mere five feet seven to her aunt's five feet ten and her mother's six feet. Nothing else did she have in common, for she was as dark as they were fair, as flat-chested as they were fulsome, and owned features as small as theirs were large.

The kitchen was a big bare room at the back of the dim central hall, its brown-painted wooden walls contributing their mite to the general atmosphere of gloominess.

"Peel the potatoes before you go out to pick the beans, Missy," said Octavia as she strapped on the voluminous brown pinny which protected her brown dress from the perils of cooking. While Missy peeled the three potatoes considered sufficient, Octavia shook up the coals smouldering in the firebox of the black iron range which occupied the whole frontage of the kitchen chimney; she then added fresh wood, adjusted the damper to cull more draught, and put a huge iron kettle on to boil. This done, she turned to the pantry to get out the raw materials for next morning's porridge.

"Oh, bother!" she exclaimed, emerging a moment later to display a brown paper bag whose bottom corners bled a flurry of oats that floated to the floor like turgid snowflakes. "Look at this! Mice!"

"Don't worry, I'll set some traps tonight," said Missy without much interest, putting her potatoes into a small pot of water, and adding a pinch of salt.

"Traps tonight doesn't get our breakfast on the table, so you'll have to ask your mother if you can run to Uncle Maxwell's to buy more oats."

"Couldn't we do without for once?" Missy hated oats.

"In *winter*?" Octavia stared at her as if she had gone mad. "A good big bowl of porridge is cheap, my girl, and sets you up for the whole day. Now hurry, for goodness sake!"

On the hall side of the kitchen door the organ music was deafening. Drusilla was an appallingly bad player who had never been told other than that she was very good, but to play with such consistent ineptitude required remorseless practice, so between four and six every weekday afternoon, Drusilla practised. There was some point to it, as she inflicted her lack of talent on the largely Hurlingford congregation at the Byron Church of England each Sunday; luckily no Hurlingford had an ear for music, so all the Hurlingfords thought they were very well served during service.

Missy crept into the parlour, not the room where they

did their handwork, but the one reserved for important occasions, and where the organ lived; there, Drusilla was assaulting Bach with all the clangour and thunder of a jousting knight his rival in the lists, seated with her back straight, her eyes closed, her head tilted, and her mouth twitching.

"Mother?" It was the smallest whisper, a filament of sound in competition against whole hawsers.

However, it was enough. Drusilla opened her eyes and turned her head, more in a spirit of resignation than anger.

"Well?"

"I'm sorry to interrupt, but we need more oats before Uncle Maxwell shuts. The mice got at the bag."

Drusilla sighed. "Bring me my purse, then."

The purse was fetched, and sixpence fished from its flaccid recesses. "*Bulk* oats, mind! All you pay for with a proprietary brand of oats is the fancy box."

"No, Mother! Proprietary oats taste much better, and you don't have to boil them all night to cook them, either." A faint hope entered Missy's breast. "In fact, if you and Aunt Octavia would rather eat proprietary oats, I'll gladly go without to make up the difference in expense."

Drusilla was always telling herself and her sister that she lived for the day her timid daughter showed signs of defiance, but this present humble bid for independence only ran up against an authoritarian wall the mother didn't know she had erected. So she said, shocked, "Go without? Most definitely not! Porridge is our winter staple, and it's a lot cheaper than coal fires." Then the tone of her voice became friendlier, more equal-women. "What's the temperature?"

Missy consulted the thermometer in the hall. "Forty-two!" she called.

"Then we'll eat in the kitchen and spend the evening there!" shouted Drusilla, beginning to give Bach another belting.

Wrapped up in her brown serge overcoat, a brown fleecy scarf and a brown knitted bonnet, with the sixpence from her mother's purse tucked down into the finger of one brown woollen glove, Missy let herself out of the house and hurried down the neat brick path to the front gate. In a small shopping bag was her library book; opportunities to sneak in an extra trip to the library were few and far between, and if she really scampered, no one need ever know she had done more than go to Uncle Maxwell's in search of oats. Tonight her Aunt Livilla would be manning the library herself, so it would have to be an improving sort of book instead of a novel, but in Missy's eyes any sort of book was better than no book at all. And next Monday Una would be there, so she could have a novel.

The air was full of a soft, fine Scotch mist that dithered between fog and rain and covered the privet hedge along the boundary of the house named Missalonghi with fat round drops of water. The moment Missy stepped out into

The Ladies of Missalonghi

Gordon Road she began to run, only slowing to a rapid walk at the corner because that wretchedly painful stitch was back in her left side, and it really did hurt. Slowing down definitely eased her discomfort, however, so she trotted along more sedately and began to experience the glow of happiness which always came when she was offered this rarest of treats, a chance to escape on her own from the confines of Missalonghi. Picking up her pace again the minute the stitch disappeared, she commenced to look around her at the familiar sights Byron had to offer on a misty late afternoon of a short winter's day.

Everything in the town of Byron was named after some aspect of the poet, including her mother's house, Missalonghi, christened after the place where Lord Byron had expired untimely. This bizarre urban nomenclature was the fault of Missy's great-grandfather, the first Sir William Hurlingford, who had founded his town hard on the heels of reading *Childe Harold*, and was so pleased that he had actually discovered a great work of literature he could understand that ever after he had rammed indigestible amounts of Byron down the throats of everyone he knew. Thus Missalonghi was situated in Gordon Road, and Gordon Road ran into Noel Street, and Noel Street ran into Byron Street, which was the main thoroughfare; on the better side of town George Street meandered for several miles before plunging over the edge of the mighty Jamieson Valley. There was even a tiny cul-de-sac called Caroline

Lamb Place, situated of course on the wrong side of the railway line (as was the house named Missalonghi); here dwelled a dozen very brassy women divided between three houses, and here came many masculine visitors from the fettlers' camp just up the line, as well as from the huge bottling plant that marred the town's southern outskirts.

It was one of the more puzzling and interesting facets of the first Sir William's intriguing character that on his deathbed he had firmly enjoined his surviving progeny not to interfere with the course of Nature by changing the function of Caroline Lamb Place, which in consequence had remained distinctly shady ever since, and not just due to its chestnut trees. In fact, the first Sir William had been addicted to what he always described as "an orderly system of naming things", and had called all his daughters by Latin names because they were popular in the higher ranks of society. His descendants kept the custom up, so there were Julias, Aurelias, Antonias, Augustas; only one branch of the family had tried to improve upon this policy by starting, with the arrival of their fifth son, to call their boys by Latin numbers, thereby glorifying the Hurlingford family tree with a Quintus, a Sextus, a Septimus, an Octavius and a Nonus. Decimus died at birth, and no one wondered at it.

Oh, how beautiful! Missy stopped to marvel at a huge spider's web beaded by the soft feelers of mist that trailed pulsating up out of the invisible valley on the far side of Gordon Road. There was a very large sleek spider at the web's middle, apologetically escorted by her tiny mate-of-the-moment, but Missy felt neither fear nor revulsion, only envy. Not merely did this lucky creature own her world intrepidly and securely, but she flew the original suffragette banner by not only dominating and using her husband, but also by eating him once his purpose was scattered over her eggs. Oh, lucky, lucky spider-lady! Demolish her world, and she would serenely remake it to inborn specifications so lovely, so ethereal, that impermanence could never matter; and when the new web was finished, she would arrange the next series of consorts upon it like a movable feast, the modestly robust husband of today just off-centre, and his successors getting littler and littler the farther they were from Mother at the hub.

The time! Missy began to run again, turning into Byron Street and heading for the row of shops which marched down either side of one block in the centre of the town, just before Byron Street became grandiose and produced the park and the railway station and the marble-fronted hotel and the imposing Egyptian façade of the Byron Waters Baths.

There was the grocery and produce store, owned by Maxwell Hurlingford; the ironmongery, owned by Denys Hurlingford; the millinery shop, owned by Aurelia Marshall, née Hurlingford; the smithy and petrol pump, owned by Thomas Hurlingford; the bakery, owned by Walter Hurlingford; the clothing emporium, owned by Herbert Hurlingford; the newsagency and stationery shop, owned by Septimus Hurlingford; the Weeping Willow Tea Room, owned by Julia Hurlingford; the lending library, owned by Livilla Hurlingford; the butchery, owned by Roger Hurlingford Witherspoon; the sweet shop and tobacconist, owned by Percival Hurlingford; and the Olympus Café and Milk Bar, owned by Nikos Theodoropoulos.

As befitted its importance, Byron Street was sealed with tarmacadam as far as its junctions with Noel Street and Caroline Lamb Place, provided with an ornate polished granite horse-trough donated by the first Sir William, and possessed of proper hitching-posts right along its awninged section of shops. It was lined with very beautiful old gum trees, and contrived to look both peaceful and prosperous.

There were very few private dwellings in the central part of Byron. The town made its living from summer visitors anxious to escape the heat and humidity of the coastal plain, and year-round visitors who aspired to ease their rheumatic aches and pains by soaking in the hot mineral waters some geological freak had placed beneath Byron ground. Therefore all along Byron Street were many guest-houses and boarding-houses – mostly owned and run by Hurlingfords, of course. The Byron Waters Baths provided a most agreeable standard of comfort for those not precisely penny-pinched, the vast and prestigious Hurlingford Hotel boasted private baths for the exclusive use of its own guests, while for those whose pecuniary resources just stretched to bed and breakfast in one of the cheaper boarding-houses, there existed the clean if spartan pools of the Byron Spa, just around the corner on Noel Street.

Even those too poor to come to the town of Byron at all were catered for. The second Sir William had invented the Byron Bottle (as it was known throughout Australia and the South Pacific); a one-pint, artistically slender, crystal-clear bottle of Byron's best spring water, gently effervescent, mildly but never disastrously aperient, distinctly tasty. Vichy water be damned! said those fortunate enough to have travelled to France. The good old Byron Bottle was not only better, it was also a great deal cheaper. And there was a penny refund on the empty too. Judicious buying of shares in the glassworks had put the final polish on this extremely inexpensive to run but remarkably lucrative local industry; it continued to thrive and to make enormous sums of money for all the male descendants of the second Sir William. The third Sir William, grandson of the first and son of the second, currently presided over the Byron Bottle Company empire with all the ruthlessness and rapaciousness of his earlier namesakes.

Maxwell Hurlingford, in direct line from the first Sir William and therefore a hugely wealthy man in his own right, did not need to run a grocery and produce store. However, commercial instinct and acumen in the Hurlingfords died hard, and the Calvinistic precepts which governed the clan dictated that a man must work to have grace in the eyes of the Lord. Rigid adherence to this rule should have made Maxwell Hurlingford a saint on earth, but instead had only managed to create a street-angel cum house-devil.

When Missy entered the shop a bell tinkled raucously, that being a perfect description of the sound Maxwell Hurlingford had devised in order to gratify his ascetics as well as his prudence. He emerged immediately the bell summoned him from the nether regions out the back, where resided the bran and chaff and wheat and barley and pollard and oats in towering stacks of hempen bags; not only did Maxwell Hurlingford cater to the gastronomic needs of the human population of Byron, he also victualled its horses, cows, pigs, sheep and chooks. As one local wit said when his grass failed, Maxwell Hurlingford got you going and coming.

His face bore its normal expression, sour, and his right hand a big scoop whiskered with webby strands of fodder.

"Look at this!" he snarled, waving the scoop at Missy in an uncanny imitation of his sister Octavia bearing her mouse-pillaged bags of oats. "Weevils all over the place."

"Oh, dear! The bulk oats too?"

"The lot."

"Then you'd better give me a box of proper breakfast oats, please, Uncle Maxwell."

"Just as well horses aren't fussy," he grumbled, putting the scoop down and squeezing behind the grocery counter.

The bell erupted into agitated life again as a man came through the door with a huge swirl of cold misty air and a dazzling briskness of purpose.

"Bloody hell, it's colder than a stepmother's tits out there!" gasped the newcomer, slapping his hands together.

"Sir! There are *ladies* present!"

"Oops!" said the newcomer, neglecting to follow this sop with an apology proper. Instead, he bellied up to the counter and grinned wickedly down at the gaping Missy. "Ladies in the plural, man? I can only see half a one!"

Neither Missy nor Uncle Maxwell could work out whether this was merely an insulting reference to her lack of height in a town of giants, or whether he was grossly insulting her by implying she was not really a lady. So by the time Uncle Maxwell had collected the use of his famously acid wits and tongue, the stranger was already well embarked upon his list of requirements.

"I want six bags of bran and pollard, a bag of flour, a bag of sugar, a box of twelve-gauge cartridges, a side of bacon, six tins of baking powder, ten pounds of tinned butter, ten pounds of raisins, a dozen tins of golden syrup, six tins of plum jam, and a ten-pound tin of Arnott's mixed biscuits."

"It is five minutes to five, and I close at five on the dot," said Uncle Maxwell stiffly.

"Then you'd better hop to it, hadn't you?" asked the stranger unsympathetically.

The box of proprietary oats was sitting on the counter;

Missy milked her sixpence out of the finger of her glove and tendered it, waiting in vain for Uncle Maxwell to give her any change and quite lacking the courage to ask him whether a small quantity of a basic commodity could cost so much, even dolled up in a fancy box. In the end she picked up the oats and left, but not before stealing another glance at the stranger.

He had a cart drawn by two horses, for such was tethered outside the store, and had not been there when Missy entered. A good-looking equipage too; the horses were trim and sleek with a sensible dash of draft in them, and the cart seemed new, the spokes of its wheels picked out in yellow on a rich brown background.

Four minutes to five. If she reversed the order of their arrival in Uncle Maxwell's shop, she could plead the stranger's rudeness and vast order as an excuse for being late, and thereby manage to fit in a dash to the library.

The town of Byron possessed no public library; few towns in Australia did in those days. But there was a privately owned lending library to fill the gap. Livilla Hurlingford was a widow with a very expensive son; economic need allied to the need always to appear respectable had driven her to open a well-stocked book room, and its popularity and profitability had led her to ignore the general blue laws which closed the shops of Byron at five on weekday afternoons, for the bulk of her patrons preferred to exchange their books in the evenings.

Books were Missy's only solace and sole luxury. She was permitted to keep the money she made from selling Missalonghi's excess eggs and butter, and she spent all of this pittance borrowing books from her Aunt Livilla's library. Both her mother and aunt disapproved strongly, but having announced some years earlier that Missy should have an opportunity to put something by above and beyond the fifty pounds her father had bestowed upon her at her birth, Drusilla and Octavia were too fair to rescind their decree simply because Missy turned out a spendthrift.

Provided she did her allotted share of the work – and did it properly, without skimping by a whisker – no one objected if Missy read books, where they objected strenuously if she voiced a desire to go walking through the bush. To walk through the bush was to place her debatably desirable person smack in the path of murder or rapine, and was not going to be permitted under any circumstances. Drusilla therefore ordered her cousin Livilla to supply Missy only with *good* books; no novels whatsoever, no scurrilous or scandalous biographies, no sort of reading matter aimed at the masculine gender. This dictum Aunt Livilla policed rigorously, having the same ideas as Drusilla about what unmarried ladies should read.

But for the last month Missy had harboured a guilty secret; she was being supplied with novels galore. Aunt Livilla had found herself an assistant to run the library on Monday and Tuesday and Saturday, thus enabling

Aunt Livilla to enjoy a four-day respite from the grizzling importunities of locals who had read everything on her shelves and visitors whose tastes her shelves did not cater for. Of course the new assistant was a Hurlingford, though not a Hurlingford from Byron; she hailed from the fleshpots of Sydney.

People rarely took any notice of the tongue-tied and sadly inhibited Missy Wright, but Una, as the new assistant was named, had seemed instantly to detect in Missy the stuff of a good friend. So from the beginning of her tenure, Una had drawn Missy out to an amazing degree; she knew Missy's habits, circumstances, prospects, troubles and dreams. She had also worked out a foolproof system whereby Missy might borrow forbidden fruit without Aunt Livilla's finding out, and she plied Missy with novels of all kinds, from the most adventurous to the most wildly romantic.

Of course tonight it would be Aunt Livilla on duty, so her book would have to be of the old kind. Yet when Missy opened the glass door and came into the cheery warmth of the book room, there sat Una behind the desk, and of the dreaded Aunt Livilla there was no sign.

More than Una's undeniable liveliness, understanding and kindness had endeared her to Missy; she was a truly remarkable looking woman as well. Her figure was excellent, her height sufficient to mark her out as a true Hurlingford, and her clothes reminded Missy of her cousin Alicia's clothes, always in good taste, always in the latest fashion, always verging on the glamorous. Arctically fair of skin and hair and eye, still Una contrived not to appear half bald and wholly washed out, which was the fate of every Hurlingford female except Alicia (who was so ravishingly beautiful that God had given her dark brows and lashes when she grew up) and Missy (who was entirely dark). Even more intriguing than Una's positive brand of fairness was a curious, luminous quality she owned, a delicious bloom that lay not so much upon her skin as inside it; her nails, oval and long, radiated this light-filled essence, as did her hair, piled in the latest puffs all around her head and culminating in a glittering topknot so blonde it was almost white. The air around her took on a sheen that was there and yet was not there. Fascinating! Lifelong exposure to none save Hurlingfords had left Missy unprepared for the phenomenon of the person with an aura; now within the space of a single little month she had met two of them, Una with her luminescence, and today the stranger in Uncle Maxwell's with his fizzy blue cloud of energy crackling around him.

"Goody!" cried Una at sight of Missy. "Darling, I have a novel you're going to adore! All about a young noblewoman of indigent means who is obliged to go governessing in the house of a duke. She falls in love with the duke and he gets her into trouble, then refuses to have anything to do with her because it's his wife has all the money. So he ships her to India, where her baby dies of cholera just after it's born.

Then this terrifically handsome maharajah sees her and falls in love with her on the spot because her hair is red-gold and her eyes are lime-green where of course all his dozens of wives and concubines are dark. He kidnaps her, intending to make her his plaything, but when he gets her into his clutches he finds out he respects her too much. So instead, he marries her and casts off all his other women because he says she is a jewel of such rarity she must have no rival. She becomes a maharanee, and very powerful. Then the duke arrives in India with his regiment of hussars to quell a native uprising in the hills, which he does, only he's fatally wounded in the battle. She takes the duke into her alabaster palace, where he finally dies in her arms, but only after she forgives him for so cruelly wronging her. And the maharajah understands at last that she really does love him more than she ever loved the duke. Isn't that a wonderful story? You'll just adore it, I promise!"

Being told the entire plot never put Missy off a book, so she accepted *Dark Love* at once and tucked it down on the bottom of her shopping bag, feeling as she did so for her own little money-purse. But it wasn't there.

"I'm afraid I've left my purse at home," she said to Una, as mortified as only someone very poor and very proud can be. "Oh, dear! I was sure I put it in! Well, you'd better have the book back until Monday."

"Lord, darling, it's not the end of the world to forget your money! Take the book now, otherwise someone else will grab it, and it's so good it'll be out for months. You can pay me next time you're in."

"Thank you," said Missy, knowing she ought not embark upon a course of action utterly against the precepts of Missalonghi, but helpless in the face of her lust for books. Smiling awkwardly, she began to back out of the shop as fast as she could.

"Don't go yet, darling," pleaded Una. "Stay and talk to me, do!"

"I'm sorry, I really can't."

"Go on, just a wee minute! Between now and seven it's as quiet as the grave, everyone's home eating tea."

"Honestly, Una, I can't," said Missy wretchedly.

Una looked mulish. "Yes, you can."

So, discovering that to refuse favours to those who held one in debt was quite impossible, Missy capitulated. "Well, all right then, but only for a minute."

"What I want to know is if you've set eyes on John Smith yet," said Una, her sparkling nails fluttering about her sparkling topknot, her blue-white eyes glowing.

"John Smith? Who's John Smith?"

"The chap who bought your valley last week."

Missy's valley was not actually her valley, of course, it simply lay along the far side of Gordon Road, but she always thought of it as hers, and had told Una more than once about her longing to walk through it. Her face fell.

"Oh, what a shame!"

"Pooh! It's a jolly good thing, if you ask me. Time someone got his foot in the Hurlingford door."

"Well, I've never heard of this John Smith, and I'm sure I've never seen him," Missy said, turning to go.

"How do you know you've never seen him when you won't even stay to hear what he looks like?"

A vision of the stranger in Uncle Maxwell's shop rose in front of Missy's eyes; she closed them and said, more positively than usual, "He's very tall and solidly built, he has curly auburn hair, an auburn beard with two streaks of white in it, his clothes are rough and he swears like a trooper. His face is nice, but his eyes are even nicer."

"That's him, that's him!" squeaked Una. "So you have seen him! Where? Tell me all!"

"He came into Uncle Maxwell's shop a few minutes ago and bought a great many supplies."

"Really? Then he must be moving into his valley." Una grinned at Missy wickedly. "I think you liked what you saw, didn't you, little Missy Sly-Boots?"

"Yes, I did," said Missy, blushing.

"So did I when I first saw him," said Una idly.

"When was that?"

"Ages ago. Years ago, in fact, darling. In Sydney."

"You *know* him?"

"Very well indeed," said Una, sighing.

The last month's spate of novels had vastly expanded

Missy's emotional education; she felt confident enough to ask, "Did you love him?"

But Una laughed. "No, darling. One thing you can be absolutely sure of, I never loved him."

"Does he come from Sydney?" asked Missy, relieved.

"Among other places."

"Was he a friend of yours?"

"No. He was a friend of my husband's."

This was news indeed to Missy. "Oh, I am sorry, Una! I had no idea you were widowed."

Una laughed again. "Darling, I am not a widow! The saints preserve me from wearing black! Wallace – my husband – is still very much alive. The best way to describe my late marriage is to say that my husband divorced himself from it – and me."

In all her life Missy had never before met a divorcée; Hurlingfords did not sunder marriages, be they made in heaven or hell or limbo. "It must have been very difficult for you," she said quietly, on her mettle not to appear prim or shocked.

"Darling, only I know how difficult it was." Una's light disappeared. "It was a marriage of convenience, actually. He found my social standing convenient – or rather his father did – and I found his pots and pots of money convenient."

"Didn't you love him?"

"My whole trouble, darling – and it has wound me up

in a lot of trouble – is that I have never loved anybody half so well as myself." She pulled a face and down went her inner light again, having just regained its normal intensity. "Mind you, Wallace was very well schooled in all the proper things, and very presentable to look at. But his father – ugh! His father was a dreadful little man who smelled of cheap pomade and even cheaper tobacco, and didn't know the first thing about manners. However, he had a burning ambition to see his son sitting right on top of the Australian heap, so he'd poured a great deal of his time and money into producing the kind of son a Hurlingford wouldn't baulk at. Where the truth was that his son liked the simple life, didn't want to sit on top of the heap, and only tried because he loved that awful old man quite desperately."

"What happened?" asked Missy.

"Wallace's father died not long after the marriage came crashing down. A lot of people reckoned the cause was a broken heart, including Wallace. As for him – I made him hate me as no man should hate any woman."

"I can't believe that," said Missy loyally.

"I daresay you genuinely can't. But it's true, all the same. Over the years since it happened, I've been forced to admit that I was a greedy selfish bitch who should have been drowned at birth."

"Oh, Una, don't!"

"Darling, don't weep for me, I'm not worth it," said Una, hard and brilliant again. "Truth's truth, that's all. So here I am, washed ashore for the very last time in a backwater like Byron, doing penance for my sins."

"And your husband?"

"He's come good. He's finally found a chance to do everything he always wanted to do."

There were at least a hundred other questions Missy was dying to ask, about Una's obvious change of heart, about the possibility she and her lost Wallace might patch things up, about John Smith, the mysterious John Smith; but the small pause which ensued after Una finished speaking brought time back with a jolt. A hasty goodbye, and she fled before Una could detain her further.

She ran almost all the five miles home, stitch or no stitch in her side, and her feet must have grown wings, for when she came breathless through the kitchen door she discovered mother and aunt perfectly ready to accept the story of John Smith's huge order as sufficient excuse for tardiness. Drusilla had milked the cow, Octavia's bones being unequal to the task, the beans were picked and simmering on the back of the range, and three lamb chops sizzled in a frying pan. The ladies of Missalonghi sat down on time to eat their dinner. And afterwards came the final chore of the day, the darning of much-laundered and much-worn stockings and underwear and linens.

Her mind half on Una's painful story and half on John Smith, Missy listened rather sleepily to Drusilla and Octavia as they indulged in their nightly dissection of whatever news might have come their news-starved way. Tonight, after an initial period of mystified discussion about the stranger in Maxwell Hurlingford's shop (Missy had not passed on what she had gleaned from Una), they proceeded to the most interesting event looming on the Byron social calendar – Alicia's wedding.

"It will have to be my brown silk, Drusilla," said Octavia, winking away a tear of wholehearted grief.

"And it will have to be my brown grosgrain, and it will have to be Missy's brown linen. Dear God, I am so tired of brown, brown, brown!" cried Drusilla.

"But in our straightened circumstances, sister, brown is the most sensible colour for us," comforted Octavia, not very successfully.

"Just once," said Drusilla savagely, jamming her needle into her reel of thread and folding the invisibly mended pillowcase with more passion than it had known in its entire long life, "I would so much like to be silly rather than sensible! As tomorrow is Saturday, I shall have to listen to Aurelia endlessly vacillating between ruby satin and sapphire velvet for her own wedding outfit, asking my opinion at least a dozen times, and I would – I would dearly love to *kill* her!"

Missy had her own room, timber-panelled and as brown as the rest of the house. The floor was covered in a mottled brown linoleum, the bed in a brown candlewick spread, the window in a brown Holland blind; there was

26

an ugly old bureau and an even older, uglier wardrobe. No mirror, no chair, no rug. But the walls did bear three pictures. One was a faded and foxed daguerrotype of an incredibly shrivelled, ancient first Sir William, taken about the time of the American Civil War; one was an embroidered sampler (Missy's earliest effort, and very well done) which announced that THE DEVIL MAKES WORK FOR IDLE HANDS; and the last was a passe-partouted Queen Alexandra, stiff and unsmiling, but still to Missy's uncritical eyes a very beautiful woman.

In the summer the room was a furnace, for it faced south of west, and in the winter it was an ice-box, taking the full brunt of the prevailing winds. No deliberate cruelty had been responsible for Missy's occupying this particular chamber; simply, she was the youngest and had drawn the shortest straw. No room in Missalonghi was truly comfortable, anyway.

Blue with cold, she shed her brown dress, her flannel petticoat, her woollen stockings and spencer and bloomers, folding them neatly before placing the underwear in a drawer and the dress on a hook in the wardrobe ceiling. Only her Sunday-best brown linen was hung up properly, for coat-hangers were very precious commodities. Missalonghi's tank held only 500 gallons, which made water the most precious commodity of all; bodies were bathed daily, the three ladies sharing the same scant bath-water, but underwear had to last two days.

Her nightgown was of prickly grey flannel, high to the neck, long-sleeved, trailing on the floor because it was one of Drusilla's hand-me-downs. But the bed was *warm*. On Missy's thirtieth birthday her mother had announced that she might have a hot brick during cold weather, since she was no longer in the first flush of youth. And when that happened, welcome though it had been, Missy abandoned forever any hope she might have cherished that she might one day find a life for herself outside the confines of Missalonghi.

Sleep came quickly, for she led a physically active life, however emotionally sterile it was. But the few moments between lying down in this blessed warmth and the onset of unconsciousness represented her only period of utter freedom, so Missy always fought sleep as long as she could.

She would begin by wondering what she really looked like. The house owned only one mirror, in the bathroom, and it was forbidden to stand and gaze at one's reflection. Thus Missy's impressions of herself were hedged with guilt that she might have stayed too long gazing. Oh, she knew she was quite tall, she knew she was far too thin, she knew her hair was straight and dark, that her eyes were black-brown, and her nose sadly out of kilter due to a fall as a child. She knew her mouth drooped down at its left corner and twisted up at its right, but she didn't know how this made her rare smiles fascinating and her normal solemn expression a clownlike tragicomedy. Life had taught her to

28

think of herself as a very homely person, yet something in her refused to believe that entirely, would not be convinced by any amount of logical evidence. So each night she would wonder what she looked like.

She would think about owning a kitten. Uncle Percival, who ran the combined sweet shop and tobacconist and was by far the nicest Hurlingford of all, had bestowed a cheeky black kitten upon her for her eleventh birthday. But her mother had taken it from her immediately and found a man to drown it, explaining to Missy with undeniable truth that they could not afford another mouth to feed, even one so small; it was not done without compassion for her daughter's feelings, nor without regret, but nevertheless it had to be done. Missy had not protested. She had not cried, either, even in her bed. Somehow the kitten had never been real enough to trigger desperate grief. But her hands could still, all these long and vacant years later, could still remember the feel of its downy fur and the vibrating thrum of its pleasure at being held. Only her hands remembered. Every other part of her had managed to forget.

She would dream of being allowed to walk through the bush in the valley opposite Missalonghi, and this was always the waking dream that passed tranquilly into sleeping dreams she could never recall. If she wore clothes they did not hamper her, nor did they get wet when she waded cascading streams, nor did they become soiled when she brushed against mossy boulders; and they were never, never brown. Bellbirds flew chiming round her head, butterflies flickered gorgeously coloured amid canopies of giant tree-ferns that made the sky seem satin under lace; everywhere was peace, nowhere did another human soul intrude.

Lately she had begun to contemplate death, who appeared to her more and more a consummation devoutly to be wished. Death was everywhere, and visited young and in-between as often as old. Consumption, fits, croup, diphtheria, growths, pneumonia, blood-poisoning, apoplexy, heart trouble, strokes. Why then should she be exclusively preserved from his hand? Death was not an unwelcome prospect at all; he never is, to those who exist rather than live.

But this night she remained wakeful through the gamut of looks, kitten, bush walks and death, in spite of an extreme weariness resulting from that scamper home and the painful stitch in her left side she seemed to be suffering more and more. For Missy had made herself save some time to devote to the big wild stranger named John Smith who had bought her valley, or so Una said. A wind of change, a new force in Byron. She believed Una was right about him, that he did intend to take up residence down in the valley. Not her valley any more; his valley now. Eyelids nearly closed, she conjured up an image of him, tall and heavy-set and strong, that lovely luxuriant dark red hair all over scalp and jaws, and two startling white ribbons in his beard. Impossible to tell his age accurately because of his weather-beaten face, though she guessed him to be somewhere on the wrong side of forty. His eyes were the colour of water that had passed over decaying leaves, crystal-clear yet amber-brown. Oh, such a *nice* man!

And when to round out this nocturnal pilgrimage she went once more upon her bush walk, he walked with her all the way into sleep.

The poverty which ruled Missalonghi with such cruel inflexibility was the fault of the first Sir William, who had sired seven sons and nine daughters, most of whom had survived to produce further progeny. It had been Sir William's policy to distribute his worldly goods among his sons only, leaving his daughters possessed of a dowry consisting of a house on five good acres of land. On the surface it seemed a good policy, discouraging fortune-hunters whilst ensuring the girls the status of land-owners as well as a measure of independence. Nothing loath (since it meant more money for them), his sons had continued the policy, and so in their turn had their sons. Only as the decades passed, the houses became steadily less commodious, less well built, and the five good acres of land tended to become five not-so-good acres of land.

The result two generations later was that the Hurlingford connection was sharply divided into several camps; uniformly wealthy males, females who were well off due to fortunate marriages, and a group of females who had either been tricked out of their land, or forced to sell it for less than its real value, or struggled still to subsist upon it, like Drusilla Hurlingford Wright.

She had married one Eustace Wright, the consumptive heir to a large Sydney accounting firm with good interests in some manufacturing concerns as well; naturally enough, at the time of her marriage she had not suspected the consumption any more indeed than had Eustace himself. But after his death only two years later, Eustace's father, surviving him, had elected to leave his property entirely to his second son rather than divert part of it to a widow with no better heir than a sickly girlchild. So what had started as an excellent essay into matrimony ended dismally in every way. Old man Wright had taken into consideration the fact that Drusilla had her house and five acres, and came from a very wealthy clan who would be obliged to look after her, if only for appearance's sake. What old man Wright failed to take into account was the indifference of the Hurlingford clan to those of its members who were female, alone, and without power.

So Drusilla eked out an existence. She had taken in her spinster sister Octavia, who sold her own house and five acres to their brother Herbert in order to contribute cash to Drusilla's household. Therein lay the rub; it was inconceivable to sell to an outsider, yet the male Hurlingfords took gross advantage of this. The ungenerous sum Herbert gave Octavia for her property was immediately invested by him on her behalf, and, as investments masterminded by

Herbert had a habit of doing, this particular one yielded absolutely nothing. The few timid enquiries Octavia had made of her brother were brushed aside at first, then treated with outraged anger and indignation.

Of course, just as it was inconceivable that any female Hurlingford should dispose of her property to an outsider, so also was it inconceivable that she should disgrace the clan by going out to work, unless work could be found for her safely within the bosom of the immediate family. Thus Drusilla, Octavia and Missy stayed at home, their utter lack of capital preventing their sanctifying work through the medium of owning a business, their utter lack of useful talents meaning the immediate family regarded them as unemployable.

Any pipe-dreams Drusilla might have harboured about Missy's growing up to snatch the ladies of Missalonghi out of penury via a spectacular marriage died before Missy turned ten; she was always homely and unprepossessing. By the time she turned twenty, her mother and her aunt had reconciled themselves to the same remorselessly straightened circumstances all the way to their respective graves. Missy in time would inherit her mother's house and five acres, but there would be none of her own to swell that, as she was a Hurlingford only on the distaff side, and therefore ineligible.

Of course they did manage to live. They had a Jersey cow which produced wonderfully rich and creamy milk as well as splendid calves, a Jersey heifer they had kept

because she was superlative, half a dozen sheep, three dozen
Rhode Island Red fowls, a dozen assorted ducks and geese,
and two pampered white sows which farrowed the best
eating-piglets in the district, as they were allowed to graze
instead of being penned up, and ate the scraps from Julia's
tea room besides the scraps from Missalonghi's table and
vegetable garden. The vegetable garden, which was Missy's
province, produced something all year round; Missy had a
green thumb. There was a modest orchard too – ten apples
of various kinds, a peach, a cherry, a plum, an apricot, and
four pear trees. Of citrus they had none, Byron being too
cold in winter. They sold their fruit and butter and eggs
to Maxwell Hurlingford for a lot less than they could have
got elsewhere, but it was inconceivable that they should sell
their produce to any but a Hurlingford.

Food they did not lack; money was what beggared them.
Prevented from earning a wage and cheated by those who
by rights should have been their greatest support, they
depended for the cash which meant clothing and utensils
and medicines and new roofs upon sale of a sheep or a calf
or a litter of piglets, and could permit of no relaxation in
their eternal financial vigilance. That Missy was dearly
loved by the two older women showed visibly in only one
way; they let her squander her egg and butter money upon
the borrowing of books.

To fill in their empty days the ladies of Missalonghi
knitted and tatted and crocheted and sewed endlessly,

grateful for the gifts of wools and threads and linens that came their way each Christmas and birthday, giving back some of the end results as their gifts in their turn, and stockpiling a great deal more in the spare room.

That they acquiesced so tamely to a regimen and a code inflicted upon them by people who had no idea of the loneliness, the bitter suffering of genteel poverty, was no evidence of lack of spirit or lack of courage. Simply, they were born and lived in a time before the great wars completed the industrial revolution, when paid work and its train of comforts were a treason to their concepts of life, of family, of femininity.

Her genteel poverty was never more galling to Drusilla Wright than each Saturday morning, when she came on foot into Byron and through it and out to where the most prosperous of the Hurlingford residences hunched across the flanks of the magnificent hills between the town and an arm of the Jamieson Valley. She went to have morning tea with her sister Aurelia, never forgetting as she trudged that when they were girls and engaged to be married, she, Drusilla, was considered to have made by far the better bargain in the matrimonial marketplace. And she made the pilgrimage alone, Octavia being too crippled to walk the seven miles, and the contrast between Missy and Aurelia's daughter Alicia too painful to be endured. Keeping a horse was out of the question, as horses were destructive grazers and Missalonghi's five acres had to be safeguarded against

35

drought at all times. If they couldn't walk, the ladies of Missalonghi stayed home.

Aurelia had also married out of the family, but far more judiciously, as things turned out. Edmund Marshall was the general manager of the bottling plant, having a talent for practical administration every Hurlingford lacked. So Aurelia lived in a twenty-roomed imitation Tudor mansion set within four acres of parkland planted with prunus and rhododendron and azalea and ornamental cherry that transformed the place into a fairyland each late September and lasted for a month. Aurelia had servants, horses, carriages, even a motorcar. Her sons Ted and Randolph were apprenticed to their father in the bottling plant and showed great promise, Ted on the accounting side and Randolph as a supervisor.

Aurelia also had a daughter, a daughter who was everything Drusilla's daughter was not. The two possessed only one fact in common; they were both thirty-three-year-old spinsters. But where Missy was as she was because no one had ever dreamed of asking her to change her single status, Alicia was still single for the most glamorous and heartrending of reasons. The fiancé she had accepted in her nineteenth year was gored to death by a maddened work elephant only weeks before their wedding, and Alicia had taken her time about recovering from the blow. Montgomery Massey had been the only child of a famous family of Ceylon tea planters, and very, very rich. Alicia had mourned him in full accordance with his social significance.

For a whole year she had worn black, then for two more years she wore only dove-grey or pale lilac, these being the colours referred to as "half-mourning"; then at twenty-two she announced the period of retirement was over by opening a millinery boutique. Her father purchased the old haberdashery shop that time and Herbert Hurlingford's clothing emporium had made redundant, and Alicia put her one genuine talent to good stead. Convention demanded that the business be placed in her mother's name, but no one, least of all her mother, was under any illusion as to whose business it was. The hat shop, called Chez Chapeau Alicia, was a resounding success from the moment it opened its doors, and drew customers from as far afield as Sydney, so delightfully attractive and flattering and fashionable were Alicia's confections in straw and tulle and silk. She employed two landless, dowerless female relations in her work room and her spinster Aunt Cornelia as her aristocratic sales dame, confining her own share of the enterprise to design and banking the profits.

Then, just when everyone had assumed that Alicia was going to wear the willow for Montgomery Massey until she too died, she announced her engagement to William Hurlingford, son and heir of the third Sir William. She was thirty-two, and her prospective bridegroom was only just nineteen. Their wedding was set for the first day of this coming October, when the spring flowers would make a garden reception *de rigueur*; the long wait would finally be over. That there had been a long wait was the fault of the third Sir William's wife, Lady Billy, who on hearing the news had attempted to flog Alicia with a horse whip. The third Sir William had been forced to forbid the couple to marry until the groom turned twenty-one.

So it was with no joy in her at all that Drusilla Wright marched up the well raked gravel drive of Mon Repos and applied the knocker to her sister's front door with a vigour born of mingled frustration and envy. The butler answered, informed Drusilla loftily that Mrs. Marshall was in the small drawing room, and conducted her there imperturbably.

The interior of Mon Repos was as charmingly right as its façade and gardens; pale imported wood panellings, silk and velvet wallpapers, brocade hangings, Axminster carpets, Regency furniture, all perfectly arranged to show off the lovely proportions of the rooms to best advantage. No need to use brown paint here, where economy and prudence so patently did not reign.

The sisters kissed cheeks, more alike in every way than either of them to Octavia or Julia or Cornelia or Augusta or Antonia, for both of them possessed a certain brand of haughty frostiness, and their smiles were identical. In spite of their contrasting social circumstances they were also more fond of each other than of any of the rest; and only Drusilla's implacable pride prevented Aurelia from assisting her financially.

After the greetings were over they settled on either side of a small marquetry table in velvet-covered chairs, and waited until the maid had served them from a tray of China tea and two dozen fairy cakes before getting down to business.

"Now it's not a scrap of use being proud, Drusilla, I do know how desperately you need the money, and can you give me one good reason why all those lovely things should pile up in your spare room instead of in Alicia's glory box? You can't plead that you're saving them for Missy's glory box when we both know Missy said her last prayers years ago. Alicia wants to buy her household linens from you, and I am in full accord," said Aurelia firmly.

"I am of course flattered," said Drusilla stiffly, "but I cannot *sell* them to you, Aurelia. Alicia may have whatever she wants as our gift."

"Nonsense!" countered the lady of the manor. "One hundred pounds, and let her take her pick."

"She may have her pick gladly, but only as our gift."

"One hundred pounds, or she will have to spend several times that buying her linens from Mark Foy's, for I will not permit her to take anything like as much as she needs from you as a gift."

The argument went on for some time, but in the end poor Drusilla was obliged to give in, her outraged pride warring with a secret relief so great it finally vanquished pride. And after she had drunk three cups of fragrant Lapsang Souchong and eaten her confection-starved way through almost the entire plate of perfectly iced pink and white fairy cakes, she and her sister had passed from the awkwardness of their social disparity to the cosiness of their social consanguinity.

"Billy says he's a jailbird," said Aurelia.

"In *Byron*? Good God, how did Billy let this happen?"

"He couldn't do a thing to prevent it, sister. You know as well as I do that it is a myth, the Hurlingfords owning every acre of land between Leura and Lawson. If the man could buy the valley, which apparently he has done, and if he has paid his debt to society, which apparently he has also done, then there is nothing Billy or anyone else can do to drive him out."

"When did all this take place?"

"Last week, according to Billy. The valley has never been Hurlingford land, of course. Billy assumed it was Crown land – a mistaken impression dating back to the first Sir William, it seems, so no one within the family has ever thought to verify the fact, more's the pity. Had we only known, a Hurlingford would have bought it long since. Actually it has been a Master of Lunacy estate for donkey's years, and then this chap bought it at auction in Sydney last week without our even learning it was for sale. The whole valley, if you please, and *dirt* cheap! Wouldn't it? Billy is livid."

"How did you find out about it?" asked Drusilla.

"The fellow arrived in Maxwell's shop yesterday just on closing time – Missy was there too, apparently."

Drusilla's face cleared. "So that's who he was!"

"Yes."

"Maxwell found out, I take it? He could prise information out of a deaf mute."

"Yes. Oh, the fellow wasn't at all backward, he talked about it very frankly – too frankly, in Maxwell's judgement. But you know Maxwell, he thinks any man a fool who advertises his business."

"What I fail to understand is why anyone other than a Hurlingford would *want* to buy the valley! I mean, to own it would have significance for a Hurlingford, because it's in Byron. But he can't farm it. It would take him ten years to clear enough to put to the plough, and it's so wet down there that he couldn't keep it cleared. He can't log it because the road out is too dangerous. So why?"

"According to Maxwell, he said he just wants to live alone in the bush and listen to the silence. Well, if he isn't actually a jailbird, you must admit he's certainly a bit of an eccentric!"

"What exactly makes Billy think he's a jailbird?"

"Maxwell phoned Billy as soon as the fellow had loaded up his cart and gone. And Billy set enquiries going at once. The fellow calls himself John Smith, if you please!" Aurelia snorted derisively. "Now I ask you, Drusilla, would anyone call himself John Smith unless there was real dirty work at the crossroads?"

"It might be his proper name," said Drusilla fairly.

"Pooh! One is forever reading about John Smiths, but have you ever actually *met* one? Billy thinks the John Smith is an – an – what do the Americans call it?"

"I haven't the faintest idea."

"Well, not that it matters, this isn't America. A false name, anyway. Billy's investigations have revealed that the man has no records with any official body. He paid in gold for the valley, and that's as much as can be found out."

"Perhaps he's a lucky strike miner from Sofala or Bendigo?"

"No. Every gold field in Australia has been in company hands for years, and there have been no big finds by a private individual, Billy says."

"How extraordinary!" said Drusilla as she absently reached for the second-last fairy cake. "Did Maxwell or Billy have anything else to add?"

"Well, John Smith bought a very large quantity of food, and he paid in gold. Out of a big money-belt under his shirt, and he not wearing an undergarment, either! Luckily by then Missy had gone, for Maxwell swears the fellow would have pulled up his shirt just the same. He *cursed* in front of Missy, *and* he said something or other that implied Missy was no lady! With *no* provocation, I assure you!"

"I believe that," said Drusilla dryly, taking the last fairy cake from the plate.

At which point Alicia Marshall came into the room. Her mother beamed at her proudly and her aunt gave her a wry

42

little smile. Why oh why couldn't Missy have been like Alicia?

A truly exquisite creature, Alicia Marshall. Very tall and built on voluptuous yet disciplined lines, she was angelically fair of skin and hair and eyes, with beautiful hands and feet, and a swanlike neck. As always, she was dressed in perfect taste, and wore her ice-blue silk gown (eyelet embroidered, its shorter overskirt fashionably pointed) with incomparable flair and grace. One of her own hats, a tumbled mass of ice-blue tulle and ice-green silk roses, adorned her profusion of palest gold hair. Miraculous, that her brows and lashes were a definite, visible brown! For naturally Alicia did not tell the world that she darkened brows and lashes any more than Una did.

"Your Aunt Drusilla would be happy to provide your household linens, Alicia," announced Aurelia triumphantly.

Alicia removed her hat and stripped off her long ice-blue kid gloves carefully, unable to answer while she concentrated on these enormously important tasks. Only when she had placed the shed articles on a table well out of harm's way and seated herself nearby did she activate her disappointingly flat and unmusical voice.

"How very kind of you, Aunt," she said.

"Kindness does not enter into it, my dear niece, since your mother is determined to pay me," said Drusilla stiffly. "You had better come to Missalonghi next Saturday morning and pick out whatever you want. I shall host morning tea."

"Thank you, Aunt."

"Shall I order some fresh tea for you?" Aurelia asked Alicia anxiously; she was just a little bit afraid of her big, capable, ambitious and driving daughter.

"No, thank you, Mother. I really came in to see what if anything you've discovered about the stranger in our midst, as Willie insists upon calling him." Her lovely lip curled.

So the news was given again and discussed again, after which Drusilla rose to go.

"Next Saturday morning at Missalonghi," she adjured her relatives, giving herself into the butler's custody.

All the way home she mentally catalogued the contents of the spare room and various cupboards, terrified that the amount and variety were not going to prove sufficient for the honest sale of one hundred pounds. One hundred pounds! What a lovely windfall! Of course it must not be *spent*. It must go into the bank and begin to accrue its minuscule interest, there to reside until disaster struck. Just what disaster, Drusilla did not know; but every blind corner on life's road concealed a disaster – illnesses, property damages and repairs, increased rates and taxes, deaths. Part of it would have to pay for the new roof, certainly, but at least they would not have to sell the Jersey heifer now to pay for that; stretched into the future with numerous as yet unconceived offspring to her credit, the Jersey heifer was worth a lot more than fifty pounds to the ladies of Missalonghi. Percival Hurlingford, a kind man with a kind wife, had always allowed them the services of his very valuable Jersey bull without charge, and had besides been responsible for the gift of their original Jersey cow.

Yes, it was most satisfactory! Perhaps Alicia, a notable trend-setter, would start a fashion among the girls of the Hurlingford connection; perhaps in future other brides-to-be would come to the ladies of Missalonghi to buy their household linens. This would be condoned as an acceptably ladylike form of business venture, where simple dressmaking would never be condoned, for that would have exposed them to the whims of anyone and everyone rather than the whims of the family.

"So, Octavia," said Drusilla to her crippled sister that night in the kitchen after they had settled to their handwork while Missy buried her head in a book, "we had better spend next week really going through everything we have, to make sure it's fit for Aurelia and Alicia to see. Missy, you will have to cope with the house and garden and animals on your own, and since you have the lightest hand with flour, you will have to make the refreshments for morning tea. We'll have pikelets with jam and cream, a sponge, some little butterfly cakes, and a sour-apple tart cooked with cloves."

This sorted out to Drusilla's satisfaction, she then passed to a spicier topic, the advent of John Smith. For once the conversation attracted Missy more than her book did, though she pretended to continue reading, and when she went to bed she carried this additional information with her to integrate and correlate among what Una had told her.

Why shouldn't his real name be John Smith? Of course the real basis for so much Hurlingford mistrust and suspicion was his acquisition of the valley. Well, John Smith, good for you! thought Missy. It's high time someone took up the Hurlingfords. She fell asleep smiling.

The fuss of preparation which preceded the visit of the two Marshall ladies was largely futile, a fact of which all three Missalonghi ladies were well aware. However, none of them minded the change of pace, for it had the virtues of novelty and misrule. Only the housebound Missy felt any pangs of regret, and her pangs were due to a combination of booklessness and fear that Una would think she had defected upon payment for the novel taken out last Friday.

The delicacies Missy had taken such pains to prepare were not eaten by the ladies for whom they were intended; Alicia "watched her figure", as she phrased it, and so too these days did her mother, who wanted to cut a figure of high fashion at her daughter's wedding. However, the goodies were not wasted upon the pigs, for later on Drusilla and Octavia gobbled them up. Though they both adored sweet things, they rarely ate them because of the additional expense.

The amount of linen displayed for Aurelia and Alicia staggered them, and after a pleasant hour spent discussing the final choices, Aurelia pressed not one but two hundred pounds into Drusilla's reluctant hand.

"No arguments, if you please!" she said, at her most imperious. "Alicia is getting a bargain."

"I think, Octavia," said Drusilla later, after the visitors had driven off in their chauffeured motorcar, "that now we can all afford new dresses for Alicia's wedding. A lilac crêpe for me, with a beaded bodice and beaded tassels around the overskirt – I have just the right beads put by! Do you remember the ones our dear mother bought to sew onto her new best half-mourning gown just before she passed away? Ideal! And I think you might purchase that powder-blue silk you so admired in Herbert's material department, don't you? Missy could tat up some lace insertions for the neck and sleeves – very smart!" Drusilla stopped to ponder, brow furrowed, looking at her dusky daughter. "You're the really difficult one, Missy. You're too dark for pale colours, so I think it will have to be..."

Oh, let it not be brown! prayed Missy. I want a *scarlet* dress! A lace dress in the sort of red that makes your eyes swim when you look at it, that's what I want!

"...brown," Drusilla finished at last, and sighed. "I understand how disappointing this must be, but the truth of the matter is, Missy, that no other colour *becomes* you half so well as brown! In pastels you look sick, in black you look jaundiced, in navy you are at death's door, and the autumn tones turn you into a Red Indian."

Missy said not a word, the logic of this being inarguable, and not knowing how much her docility pained Drusilla,

47

who would have welcomed a suggestion at least – though of course scarlet would not have been countenanced under any circumstances. It was the colour of tarts and trollops, fully as much as brown was the colour of the respectable poor.

However, nothing could keep Drusilla's spirits oppressed for long tonight, so she cheered up again rapidly. "In fact," she said happily, "I think we can all have new boots as well. Oh, what a dash we're going to cut at the wedding!"

"Shoes," said Missy suddenly.

Drusilla looked blank. "*Shoes?*"

"Not boots, Mother, please! Let us have shoes, pretty dainty shoes with Louis heels and bows on the front."

It is possible that Drusilla may have considered the idea, but Missy's cry from the heart was smothered immediately by Octavia, who, in her invalidish way, did quite a lot of the ruling at the house called Missalonghi.

"Living all the way out at the end of Gordon Road?" Octavia snorted. "You're not right in the head, girl! Just how long do you think shoes would last in the dust and the mud? Boots are what we must have, good sturdy boots with good sturdy laces and good sturdy thick heels on them. Boots *last*! Shoes are not for those who must go on Shank's pony."

And that was that.

By the Monday following the visit of Aurelia and Alicia Marshall, life had returned to normal at Missalonghi, so Missy was allowed to take her habitual walk to the lending library in Byron. Of course it wasn't all selfish pleasure; she went armed with two large shopping bags, one for either hand to balance the load, and she did the week's marketing as well.

Quiescent for the week she had stayed at home, the stitch in Missy's side came back in full force. Odd, that it only seemed to bother her on long walks. And it was painful, so wretchedly painful!

Today her own purse had joined company with her mother's, and her mother's purse was unusually fat, for Missy had been commissioned to buy the lilac crêpe and the powder-blue silk and her own brown satin at Herbert Hurlingford's clothing emporium.

Of all the shops in Byron, Missy hated Uncle Herbert's the most, for he staffed it exclusively with young men, sons or grandsons naturally; even if one were purchasing stays or under-drawers, one had to suffer the attentions of a sniggering cad who found his task exquisitely funny and his customer the embarrassed butt of his jokes. However, this sort of treatment was not meted out to everyone, only to those whose means were sufficiently pinched to make shopping in Katoomba or – God forbid! – Sydney an impossibility; it was also chiefly reserved for Hurlingford women who had no men to exact retribution. Old maids and indigent widows of the clan were uniformly regarded as fair game.

As she stood watching James Hurlingford bring down the bolts she indicated, Missy wondered what he would have done had her own brown satin been a request for scarlet lace. Not that the clothing emporium stocked such a fabric; the only reds it offered were cheap and vulgar artificial silks kept for the denizens of Caroline Lamb Place. So along with the lilac crêpe and the powder-blue silk, Missy bought a length of very beautiful delustred satin in the shade known as snuff. Had the material been any other colour she would have loved it, but since it was brown, it may as well have been jute sacking. Every dress Missy had ever owned had been brown; it was such a serviceable colour. Never showed the dirt, never went in or out of fashion, never faded, never looked cheap or common or trollopy.

"New dresses for the wedding?" asked James archly.

"Yes," said Missy, wondering why it was that James always succeeded in making her feel so uncomfortable; perhaps it was his exaggeratedly womanish manner?

"Let's see, now," burbled James, "how about a weeny game of guessies? The crêpe is for Auntie Drusie, and the silk is for Auntie Octie, and the satin – the *brown* satin – must therefore be for little brown Cousin Missy!"

Her brain must still have been filled with the image of that impossible scarlet lace dress, for quite suddenly Missy saw nothing but scarlet, and out of the recesses of her memory she dredged the only insulting phrase she knew.

"Oh, go bite your bum, James!" she snapped.

He would not have been so shocked had his wooden dress dummy come to life and kissed him, and he measured and he cut with a hitherto unknown alacrity, thereby unintentionally giving each lady an extra yard of fabric, and he couldn't get Missy out of the shop fast enough. The pity was that he knew he couldn't confide his dreadful experience to any of his brothers or nephews, because they would probably echo Missy's words, the bastards.

The library was only two doors down, so when Missy went in she was still flying the flags of her anger in her cheeks, and she banged the door after her.

Una looked up, startled, and began to laugh. "Darling, you look absolutely splendid! In a paddy, are we?"

Missy took a couple of deep breaths to calm down. "Oh, just my cousin James Hurlingford. I told him to go bite his bum."

"Good for you! Time someone told him." Una giggled. "Though I imagine he'd much rather someone else bit it for him – preferably someone masculine."

This sailed straight over Missy's head, but Una's burst of merriment did the trick, and Missy found herself able to laugh too. "Dear oh dear, it wasn't very ladylike of me, was it?" she asked, sounding more surprised than horrified. "I don't know what came over me!"

The radiant face turned up to her looked suddenly sly, not the slyness of dishonesty but the slyness of someone fey, away with the fairies. "Straws and camels," intoned Una in a singsong voice, "eyes of needles and days of dogs, revolving worms and well reaped whirlwinds. There's a lot in you,

Missy Wright, that you don't even know is there." She sat back and hummed like a gleeful naughty child. "But it's started now, and it can't be stopped."

Out came the story of the scarlet lace dress, the terrible longing to wear something other than brown, the defeat of having to admit no other colour than brown suited her, so that on this glorious day when she might actually have attained a dress in some other colour, still she must wear brown. Her feyness quite vanished, Una listened sympathetically, and when Missy had got it all out of her system, she looked her up and down deliberately.

"Scarlet *would* suit you beautifully," she said. "Oh, what a pity! Still, never mind, never mind." And she changed the subject. "I've saved another new novel for you – two pages into it, and I promise you won't even remember your red dress. It's all about a drab young woman who is utterly downtrodden by her family until the day she finds out she's dying of heart trouble. There's this chap she's been in love with for years, only of course he's engaged to someone else. So she takes the letter from the heart specialist telling her she's going to die to this young man, and she begs him to marry her rather than the other girl, because she's only got six months to live and after she's dead he can marry the other girl anyway. He's a bit of a wastrel, but he's just waiting for someone to reform him, only he doesn't know that, naturally. Anyway, he agrees to marry her. And they have six heavenly months together. He finds out that under her drab exterior she's an entrancing person, and her love for him reforms him completely. Then one day when the sun is shining and the birds are singing, she dies in his arms – I love books where people die in each other's arms, don't you? – and his old fiancée comes round to see him after the funeral because she got a letter from his dead wife explaining why he jilted her. And his old fiancée says she forgives him and she'll marry him the minute he's out of mourning. But he jumps up, wild with grief, rushes to the river and throws himself in, calling out his dead wife's name. And then his old fiancée throws herself in the river, calling out his name. Oh, Missy, it's so sad! I cried for days."

"I'll take it," said Missy instantly, paid up all her debts, which made her feel a lot better, and tucked *The Troubled Heart* into the bottom of one of her shopping bags.

"I'll see you next Monday," said Una, and went to the door to wave at her until she disappeared from sight.

As long as she walked it on her own, the five miles from Byron's shops to Missalonghi never seemed half so much. For as she walked, she dreamed, fantasising herself into roles and events and characters far beyond her real ken. Until Una had come to the library these characters had all looked exactly like Alicia, and the antics they got up to revolved around hat shops or dress shops or tea rooms of awesome gentility, and the men in their lives were a composite Hurlingford beau ideal, Siegfrieds in boots, bowlers, and three-piece suits. Nowadays her imagination had better grist to work on, and whatever character she played through whatever adventure it might be bore far more resemblance to the latest novel Una had smuggled her than to any aspect of Byron life.

So for the first half of her walk home that Monday, Missy metamorphosised herself into a divinely beautiful strawberry blonde with amazing lime-green eyes; she had two men in love with her, a duke (fair and handsome), and an Indian prince (dark and handsome). In this guise she shot tigers down from the howdahs of richly caparisoned elephants without assistance, she led an army of her husband's subjects against Muslim marauders without assistance, she built schools and hospitals and mothers' institutes without assistance, while her two lovers drifted vaguely in the background rather like the little male spider consorts not permitted into the wife's parlour.

But halfway home, where Gordon Road branched off from the long straggle of Noel Street, began her valley. At this point Missy always stopped daydreaming and looked about her instead. It was a beautiful day, as late winter days on the Blue Mountains can be when the wind takes time off to rest. Answering the lure of the valley, she crossed to the far side of Gordon Road and lifted her face to the kindly sky and swelled her nostrils to take in the heady tang of the bush.

No one had ever produced a name for the valley, though from now on it would in the way of Byron folk come to be known as John Smith's Valley, no doubt. Compared to the Jamieson Valley or the Grose Valley or even the Megalong

Valley it was not very big, but it was perfect, a bowl some fifteen hundred feet lower than the three thousand foot ridge upon which Byron and all the other towns of the Blue Mountains were built. In shape it was a symmetrical oval, one narrow curving end lying just beyond the place where Gordon Road petered out and the far end some five miles away to the east, where its otherwise uninterrupted wall was dramatically broken by a chasm through which flowed its nameless river on its way to join the Nepean-Hawkesbury system of the coastal plain. All the way round the margin was a stunning drop of dull orange sandstone cliff a thousand feet high, and below this sheer precipice a tree-covered skirt of fallen rock curved down to the course of the river which had made the valley aeons before. And the valley was, looking across it, stuffed with lush native forest, a blue ocean of gums that sighed and whispered ceaselessly.

On winter mornings the valley was filled with brilliant white cloud that sat like turning milk below the level of the cliff tops, and suddenly as the sun increased in warmth it would lift up in a moment and vanish. Sometimes the cloud would come down from above, fingers seeking out the tree tops far below until it succeeded in covering them from sight under a spectral blanket. And as sunset approached, winter and summer, the cliffs began to take on deeper, richer colour, glowering rose-red, then crimson, and finally the purple that faded into night's mysterious indigo. Most wonderful of all was the rare snow, when all the crags and outcrops of the cliffs were picked out in white, and the moving leafy trees shook off their powdering of icy moisture as fast as it fell upon them, unwilling to accept a touch so alien.

The only way down to the valley's floor was a terrifyingly steep track just wide enough for a large wagon, a track that emerged onto the top of the rim just beyond the end of Gordon Road. Fifty years earlier, someone had made the track in order to plunder the rainforest below of its massive cedars and turpentines, but after a whole team of eighty oxen, their driver, two loggers and a dray bearing a mighty tree trunk had gone over the edge, the plundering had ceased abruptly. There were easier forests to log. And gradually the track had been forgotten, as indeed had the valley; visitors preferred to go south to the Jamieson than north to this less awesome cousin, bereft as it was of kiosks and properly landscaped lookouts.

That wretched stitch came back just as Missy rounded the corner not far from Missalonghi, and ten seconds later the pain struck at her chest like a blow from an axe. She faltered and dropped her loaded shopping bags, her arms flying up to pluck at this terrifying agony; then she saw the neat hedge of Missalonghi through her terror, and ran for home. At precisely the same moment John Smith rounded the corner from its other side, striding along with his head down in thought.

Only ten yards short of the gate in the hedge, she pitched

headlong. No one inside Missalonghi saw, for it was about five o'clock, and the rolling chords of Drusilla's organ were erupting into the outside air like a suffocating fall of hot volcanic ash.

But John Smith saw, and came running. His first thought was that the odd little soul had tripped after bolting to escape meeting him, but when he knelt and turned her face upwards, one look at her grey skin and sweat-soaked hair told him differently. He half-sat her against his thigh, rubbing her back helplessly, wishing he knew of some way to force air into her lungs. That much knowledge he had, not to lie her flat on the ground, yet farther than that his knowledge did not extend. She put up her hands to clutch at his arm where it lay lightly across the front of her shoulders, supporting her; the whole of her body was heaving with the fight to breathe, and her eyes were turned up to his, silently beseeching him for an aid he was incapable of giving. Caught mesmerised, watching the extraordinary cavalcade of an inner horror and bewilderment and pain pass through those eyes, he began to think she was going to die.

Then with startling swiftness the grey colour faded, a warmer and healthier tinge crept into her skin, and her hands relaxed on his arm.

"Please!" she gasped, struggling to rise.

He got to his feet at once, slipped one arm under her legs and scooped her up. Though he had no idea where she lived, there must surely be some assistance in the dingy house behind the hedge, so he carried her through the gate and down the path, calling for help at the top of his voice and praying he would be heard above the bellowing of the organ.

Apparently he was heard, for two ladies came out of the house immediately, both unknown to him. There was no nonsense about them, which he appreciated deeply; one pointed wordlessly to the front door, while the other slipped around ahead of him and ushered him into the parlour with his burden.

"Brandy," said Drusilla curtly, bending to loosen her daughter's clothes. She wore no stays, having no need of them, but her dress was tightly belted and high to the neck.

"Do you have a telephone?" asked John Smith.

"I'm afraid not."

"Then if you give me directions, I'll go for the doctor right now."

"The corner of Byron and Noel, Dr. Neville Hurlingford," said Drusilla. "Tell him it's Missy – she's my daughter."

He went immediately, leaving Drusilla and Octavia to administer the brandy every prudent household kept in the sauce cupboard in case of heart trouble.

By the time Dr. Neville Hurlingford arrived some sixty minutes later, Missy had almost fully recovered. John Smith did not return with him.

"Very puzzling," said Dr. Hurlingford to Drusilla in the kitchen; Octavia was helping Missy into bed.

The experience had shaken Drusilla badly, used to

assuming that everyone she knew enjoyed the same rude health she did herself; Octavia's bones were such old friends they didn't really count. So soberly and quietly she made a pot of tea, and drank from her own cup more gratefully than Dr. Hurlingford did from his.

"Did Mr. Smith tell you what happened?" she asked.

"I must say, Drusilla, that in spite of the tall stories going around at the moment, Mr. Smith seems to me to be a good fellow – a sensible and practical man. According to him, she grabbed at her chest, ran across the road in a panic, and collapsed. She was grey and sweating and having great trouble breathing. The attack lasted about two minutes, and her recovery was quite sudden. Her colour came back, so did her breath. That was when Mr. Smith brought her inside, I gather. I could find nothing wrong with her a minute ago, but I may find more when I do a proper examination once she's in bed."

"There's no heart trouble in our branch of the family, as you know," said Drusilla, feeling betrayed.

"She takes after her father's family in the rest of her bodily makeup, Drusilla, so she may have inherited a bad heart from that side too. She has had no other attack like it?"

"Not that we know of," said Drusilla, properly rebuked. "*Is* it her heart?"

"I honestly don't know. It's possible." But he sounded doubtful. "I'll go in and see her again now, I think."

Missy was lying in her narrow little bed with her

eyes closed, but the moment she heard Dr. Hurlingford's unfamiliar step she opened them and looked at him, then unaccountably seemed disappointed.

"Well now, Missy," he said, sitting gingerly alongside her. "What happened, eh?"

Drusilla and Octavia hovered in the background; he would dearly have liked to dismiss them, sensing that their presence inhibited Missy, but decency and convention forbade it. In all of Missy's life he had only seen her two or three times, so he knew only the little about her that everyone knew; she was the sole dark Hurlingford in history, and she had been doomed to spinsterhood before she was into her teens.

"I don't know what happened," lied Missy.

"Come now, you must remember something."

"I got short of breath and fainted, I suppose."

"That's not what Mr. Smith says."

"Then Mr. Smith is wrong – where is he? Is he here?"

"Did you experience any pain?" pressed Dr. Hurlingford, not satisfied, and not bothering to answer Missy's question.

A ghastly vision of herself reduced to the status of a chronic invalid at Missalonghi rose up in front of Missy's mind; the awful additional monetary burden she would become, the guilt she would in consequence feel every day of her bedbound life, the impossibility of ever getting away on her own to walk past her valley into Byron and the library – no, it could not be borne!

"I had no pain at all," she insisted.

Dr. Hurlingford looked as if he didn't believe her, but for a Hurlingford he was fairly perceptive, and he too knew what sort of life Missy would lead from the moment she was diagnosed a case of heart trouble. So he forebore to press the poor girl further, merely got out his old-fashioned funnel-shaped stethoscope and listened to her heart, which was beating quite normally, and to her lungs, which were clear.

"Today is Monday. You had better come and see me on Friday," he said as he rose. He patted Missy reassuringly on top of her head and then walked into the hall, where Drusilla lurked in wait. "I can't find anything wrong," he said to her. "Lord knows what happened, I don't! But mind she sees me on Friday, now, and if anything else happens in the meantime, send for me at once."

"No medicine?"

"My dear Drusilla, how can I prescribe medicine for a mystery illness? She's as skinny as a wormy cow, but she seems healthy enough. Just leave her alone, let her sleep, and give her plenty of good nourishing food."

"Should she stay in bed until Friday?"

"I don't think so. Let her stay in bed tonight, but let her get up tomorrow. Provided she only does light duties, I can see no harm in her leading a normal and active life."

With that Drusilla had to be satisfied. She ushered her uncle the doctor out, tiptoed across the hall to the door of Missy's room and peeped in, saw that Missy was asleep, and so retreated to the kitchen, where Octavia was sitting at the table polishing off the last of the doctor's pot of tea.

Actually Octavia looked very shaken; the hands that both were needed to lift her cup to her lips trembled badly.

"Uncle Neville doesn't seem to think it's serious," said Drusilla, sitting down heavily. "Missy is to stay in bed for what's left of this evening, but she can get up tomorrow and move around, though only light duties until Uncle sees her again on Friday."

"Oh, dear!" A large pale tear rolled down Octavia's large pale cheek as she looked down at her gnarled fingers. "I will try in the garden, Drusilla, but I really cannot milk the cow!"

"I'll milk," said Drusilla. She put her hand to her head and sighed. "Don't worry, sister, we'll manage somehow."

The disaster! Drusilla saw her precious two hundred pounds frittering itself away on a series of doctors and hospitals and treatments, none of which would she grudge for a moment; what depressed her was the disappearance of her tail just when she thought she had caught up with it at last. If she had not already cut out the lilac crêpe and the powder-blue silk and the snuff-brown satin, back they would have gone to Herbert's emporium on the morrow. *Wouldn't* it?

At dinner time Drusilla brought Missy a huge bowl of beef-and-barley broth and sat by the bed until Missy managed to struggle through it; but after that she was left mercifully alone. The long sleep of the earlier part of the evening had left her wakeful, though, so she settled to think. About the pain and what it might mean. About John Smith. About the future. Between the pain and the future, two deserts of appalling dreariness, John Smith stood lit up and glorious. So she abandoned all thought of pain or future, and concentrated upon John Smith.

Such a nice man! Interesting too. How easily he had lifted her off the ground and carried her inside. The recent avalanche of second-hand knowledge Una's smuggled novels had tipped on top of her was suddenly of genuine benefit; Missy understood that she was in love at last. But hope was not present at all in the sweet and smiling train of thought this realisation of love triggered. The Alicias of this world might scheme and plot to attain their ends, but the Missys could not. The Missys didn't know enough about men, and the smidgin they did know lay in the realm of generality. All men were untouchables, even jailbirds. All men had choices. All men had power. All men were free. All men were privileged. And presumably jailbirds had more of everything than men like poor Little Willie Hurlingford, sheltered as he had been from every adverse wind that might have blown a little stiffening into him. Not that she believed John Smith was really a jailbird; Una had known him during her years in Sydney, and presumably that meant he had moved at least on the fringes of the highest society – unless of course despite his friendship with Una's husband he had delivered the ice, or the bread, or the coal.

Oh, but he had been nice to her! Nice to a nonentity like Missy Wright. Even through that hideous and frightening pain she had been conscious of his presence, felt too some strange passage of strength from him to her that had, she fancied, tossed death aside like so much chaff.

John Smith, she thought, if I were only young and pretty, you would stand no more chance of escaping me than poor Little Willie did Alicia! I would chase you remorselessly until I caught you. Wherever you went, there I would be, with my best foot forward to trip you up. And once I had you in my toils, I would love you so much and so well that you would never, never want to get away from me.

John Smith came in person the next day to enquire after Missy, but Drusilla dealt with him at the front door and did not permit him sight or sound of Missy. It was merely a courtesy call, as Drusilla perfectly understood, so she thanked him nicely but not profusely and then stood watching as he strode off down the path to the gate with his hands swinging loosely and his lips whistling a saucy tune.

"Fancy that!" said Octavia, coming out of the parlour, where she had been hiding to watch John Smith through a lifted curtain edge. "Are you going to tell Missy he called?"

"Why?" asked Drusilla, surprised.

"Oh, well..."

"My dear Octavia, you sound as if you've been reading those penny dreadful romances Missy's been bringing home from the library recently!"

"*Has* she?"

Drusilla laughed. "You know, until I realised what a dither she was in trying to hide the covers of her books, I'd forgotten all about our original rule as to the kind of books she might read. After all, it was fifteen years ago! And I thought, why should the poor little wretch not read romances if she wants? What has she to enjoy the way I enjoy my music?"

Nobly Drusilla refrained from adding that Octavia had her rheumatics to enjoy, and Octavia, who might under different circumstances have implied aloud how bereft she herself was of things to enjoy, wisely decided to leave the subject of enjoyment alone.

"Aren't you going to tell her she may read romances?" Octavia asked instead.

"Certainly not! If I did that, it would remove most of her pleasure, you know. Pure freedom to read them would only give her sufficient detachment to see how dreadful they are." Drusilla frowned. "What intrigues me is how Missy managed to persuade Livilla of all people to let her borrow them. But I can't ask Livilla without letting the cat out of the bag, and I wouldn't spoil Missy's fun for the world. I see it as a wee bit of defiance, and that gives me hope that there's some starch in Missy's backbone after all."

Octavia sniffed. "I can't see anything laudable about a sort of defiance that necessitates her becoming *under-handed*!"

A small sound halfway between a growl and a mew escaped Drusilla's lips, but then she smiled, shrugged, and led the way into the kitchen.

Drusilla accompanied Missy to the doctor the following Friday morning. They went off on foot in good time, warmly clad – naturally – in brown.

The surgery waiting room, dim and fusty, was empty. Mrs. Neville Hurlingford, who did service as her husband's nurse, ushered them into it with a cheery word for Drusilla and a rather blank stare for Missy. A moment later, the doctor poked his head round his consulting room door.

"Come in, Missy. No, Drusilla, you can stay there and talk to your aunt."

Missy went in, sat down, and waited warily, her guard up.

He commenced with a frontal attack. "I do not believe you were merely short of breath," he said. "There had to be pain, and I want to hear all about it, and no nonsense."

Missy gave in, told him about the stitch in her left side, the way it only bothered her on long walks if she hurried, and the way it had ushered in that sudden, terrifying onslaught of severe pain and breathlessness.

So he examined her again, and afterwards sighed. "I can find absolutely nothing the matter with you," he said. "When I examined you last Monday there were no residual signs to indicate heart trouble, and today is the same. However, from what Mr. Smith told me, you certainly did have some sort of genuine turn. So, just to make sure, I'm going to send you to a specialist in Sydney. If I can arrange an appointment, would you like to go down with Alicia on her weekly Tuesday trip to the city? It would save your mother having to go."

Was there an understanding twinkle in his eyes? Missy wasn't sure, but she looked at him gratefully all the same. "Thank you, I'd like to go with Alicia."

In fact, Friday was a very good day, for in the afternoon Una drove up to Missalonghi in Livilla's horse and sulky, and she had half a dozen novels with her, discreetly wrapped in plain brown paper.

"I didn't even know you were ill until Mrs. Neville Hurlingford told me this morning in the library," she said, sitting down in the best parlour, to which Octavia had ushered her, dazzled by her elegance and composure.

Neither Drusilla nor Octavia offered to let the two young women talk alone, not because they were consciously spoil-sporting, but because they were always starved for company, especially when the company took the form of a brand new face. Such a lovely face too! Not beautiful like Alicia, yet – disloyal though the thought was, they fancied Una was perhaps the more alluring of the two. Her arrival pleased Drusilla particularly, since it answered the vexed question as to how Missy was suddenly managing to borrow novels.

"Thank you for the books," said Missy, smiling at her friend. "The one I brought home last Monday is nearly worn out."

"Did you enjoy it?" asked Una.

"Oh, very much!" As indeed she had; its dying heroine with her dicky heart could not have come at a more appropriate moment. Admittedly the heroine actually had managed to die in her beloved's arms, but she, Missy, had had the good fortune merely *almost* to die in her beloved's arms.

Una's manners were perfect. By the time she had partaken of a cup of tea and some plain home-made biscuits, she had won Drusilla and Octavia over completely. To have no better fare to offer was humiliating, but Una's appreciation turned the despised biscuits into an inspired guess as to what the visitor really liked and wanted.

"Oh, I get so tired of cream cakes and asparagus rolls!" she exclaimed, smiling with dazzling effect at her hostesses. "How clever of you, and how considerate! These little biscuits are delicious, and *so* much better for my digestion! Most Byron ladies swamp one in oceans of jam and cream, and as a guest it is of course impossible to refuse refreshments without offending."

"What a lovely person," said Drusilla after Una had gone.

"Delightful," agreed Octavia.

"She may come again," said Drusilla to Missy.

"Any time," said Octavia, who had made the biscuits.

On Sunday afternoon Missy announced that she didn't care to read, she was going for a walk in the bush instead.

So calm and decided was her tone that for a moment her mother just stared at her, at a loss.

"A walk?" she asked at last. "In the *bush*? Most definitely not! You don't know who you might meet."

"I won't meet anyone," said Missy patiently. "There has never been any kind of prowler or molester of women in Byron."

Octavia pounced. "How do you know there's never been a prowler, madam? It's that ounce of prevention, and never do you forget it! If a prowler is prowling hereabouts, he never finds anyone to molest, because we Hurlingfords keep our girls safe at home, which is where you ought to be."

"If you are set on the idea, then I suppose I must come with you," said Drusilla in the tones of a martyr.

Missy laughed. "Oh, Mother! Come with me when you're so engrossed in your beading? No, I'm going on my own, and that's final."

She walked out of the house wearing neither overcoat nor scarf to protect her from the wind.

Drusilla and Octavia looked at each other.

"I hope her brain's not affected," said Octavia dolefully.

So secretly did Drusilla, but aloud she said stoutly, "At least you can't call this bit of defiance *underhanded*!"

In the meantime Missy had let herself out of the front gate and turned left instead of right, down to where Gordon Road dwindled to two faint wheel-marks meandering into the heart of the bush. A glance behind her revealed that no one was following; Missalonghi's squat ugliness sat with front door firmly closed.

It was a still clear day and the sun was very warm, even filtering through the trees. Up here on top of the ridge the bush was not thick, for the soil was scanty and whatever did grow mostly had to scrabble for an unloving hold on the sandstone substrate. So the eucalypts and angophoras were short, stunted, and the undergrowth sparse. Spring had arrived; even high up in the Blue Mountains it came early, and two or three warmish days were sufficient to bring the first wattle popping out into a drift of tiny fluffy yellow balls.

The valley went on to her right, glimpsed through the trees; where was John Smith's house, if house he had? Her mother's Saturday morning visit to Aunt Aurelia's yesterday had elicited no further information about John Smith, save a wild rumour that he had engaged a firm of Sydney builders to erect him a huge mansion at the bottom of the cliffs, made out of sandstone quarried on the spot. But Missalonghi could offer no evidence to support this, and Missalonghi sat plump on the only route such builders would have to use. Besides which, Aunt Aurelia apparently had more important worries than John Smith; it seemed the upper echelons of the Byron Bottle Company were becoming extremely alarmed about some mysterious movements in shares.

Missy had no expectation of meeting John Smith on top of the ridge, as it was Sunday, so she decided to find out where his road went over the edge of the valley. When at last she stumbled upon the spot she could see the logic behind the site, for a gargantuan landslide had strewn boulders and rocks in a kind of ramp from top to bottom of the cliff, thus decreasing the sheerness of the drop. Standing at the commencement of the track, she could just glimpse it twisting back and forth across the landslide in a series of zigzags; a perilous descent, yes, but not an impossible one for a cart like John Smith's.

However, she was far too timid to venture down, not from fear of falling but from fear of walking into John Smith's lair. Instead, she struck off into the bush on top of the ridge along a narrow path that might have been made by animals going to water. And sure enough, as time went by a sound of running water gradually overpowered the omnipresent sound of the trees talking in that faint, plaintive, fatigued speech gum trees produce on calm days. Louder and louder was the water, until it became a bewildering roar; then when she came upon the stream, it offered her no answer, for though it was quite deep and wide, it was sliding along between its ferny banks without a flurry. Yet the roar of rushing water persisted.

She turned to the right and followed the river, inside her dream of enchantment at last. The sun glanced off the surface of the water in a thousand thousand sparks of light, and the ferns dripped tiny droplets, and dragonflies hovered with rainbow-mica wings, and brilliant parrots wheeled from the trees of one bank to the trees of the other.

Suddenly the river vanished. It just fell away into nothing, a smoothly curving edge. Gasping, Missy drew back quickly, understanding the roar. She had come to the very head of the valley, and the stream which had cut it was entering it in the only way possible, by going down, down, down. Working cautiously along the brink for a good quarter of a mile, she came to a place where a great rock jutted far out over the cliff. And there, right on its end, legs dangling into nothingness, she sat to watch the waterfall in awe. Its bottom she could not discover, only the beautiful untidy tangle of its flight through the windy air, and a rainbow against a mossy place on the cliff behind it, and a chilly moistness that it exhaled as it fell, like a cry for help.

Several hours slipped away as easily as the water. The sun left that part of the ridge. She began to shiver; time to go home to Missalonghi.

And then where her path joined the road leading down into John Smith's valley, Missy met John Smith himself. He was driving his cart from the direction of Byron, and she saw with surprise that the cart was laden with tools and crates and sacks and iron machinery. Somewhere was a shop open on Sunday!

He pulled up at once and jumped down, smiling broadly. "Hello!" he said. "Feeling better?"

"Yes, thank you."

"I'm glad to catch you like this, because I was beginning to wonder if you were still in the land of the living. Your mother assured me you were when I called, but she wouldn't let me see for myself."

"You came to see how I was?"

"Yes, last Tuesday."

"Oh, thank you for that!" she said with fervour.

His brows rose, but he didn't attempt to quiz her. Instead, he left his conveyance where it was, and turned to walk back with her towards Missalonghi.

"I take it there was nothing serious wrong?" he asked after some minutes during which they just paced along together without speaking.

"I don't know," said Missy, recognising the emanations of pity and sympathy his obviously healthy being was giving off. "I have to see a doctor in Sydney quite urgently. A *heart* specialist, I believe." Now why did she say it like that?

"Oh," he said, at a loss.

"Whereabouts exactly do you live, Mr. Smith?" she asked, to change the subject.

"Well, further around in the direction you've just come from is a waterfall," he said, not at all reticently, and in a tone of voice which told Missy that, whether because of her sickly condition or because maybe she was so manifestly harmless, he had decided she could be counted a friend. "There's an old logger's hut near the bottom of the waterfall, and I'm camping in that for the time being. But I'm starting to build a house a bit closer to the waterfall itself – out of sandstone blocks I'm quarrying on the site. I've just been down to Sydney to pick up an engine to drive a big saw. That way I can cut my blocks a lot faster and better, and mill my own timber too."

She closed her eyes and heaved a big unconscious sigh. "Oh, how I envy you!"

He stared down at her curiously. "That's an odd thing for a woman to say."

Missy opened her eyes. "Is it?"

"Women usually don't like being cut off from shops and houses and other women." His tone was hard.

"You're probably right for the most part," she said thoughtfully, "but in that sense I don't really count as a woman, so I envy you. The peace, the freedom, the isolation – I dream of them!"

The end of the track came into sight, and so did the faded red corrugated iron roof of Missalonghi.

"Do you do all your shopping in Sydney?" she asked, for something to say, then chastised herself for asking a silly question; hadn't she met him first in Uncle Maxwell's?

"I do when I can," he said, obviously not connecting her with Uncle Maxwell's, "but it's a long haul up the Mountains with a full load, and I've got only this one team of horses. Still, Sydney's definitely preferable to shopping in Byron – I've never encountered a place so full of Nosey Parkers."

Missy grinned. "Try not to blame them too much, Mr. Smith. Not only are you a novelty, but you've also stolen what they have always regarded as their exclusive property, even if they never thought about it, or wanted it."

He burst out laughing, evidently tickled that she should bring the matter up. "My valley, you mean? They could have bought it, the sale wasn't secret – it was advertised in the Sydney papers and in the Katoomba paper. But they're just not as smart as they think they are, that's all."

"You must feel like a king down there."

"I do, Miss Wright." And he smiled at her, tipped his battered bushman's hat, turned and walked away.

Missy floated the rest of the way home, in perfect time to milk the cow. Neither Drusilla nor Octavia made reference to her bush walk, Drusilla because she had been more pleased at the display of independence than worried about the outcome, and Octavia because she had convinced herself Missy's cerebral processes were being affected by whatever ailed her.

In fact, when by four o'clock there had been no sign of Missy, the two ladies left at Missalonghi had had a small tiff. Octavia thought it was time to inform the police.

"No, no, no!" said Drusilla, quite violently.

"But we must, Drusilla. Her brain's affected, I know it is. When in her whole life has she ever behaved this way?"

"I have been thinking ever since Missy had her turn, sister, and I'm not ashamed to say that when Mr. Smith carried her in, I was terrified. The thought of losing her to such an unfair, unjust thing – I was never more glad than when Uncle Neville told me he didn't think it was serious. And then I began to wonder what would happen to Missy had it been me? Octavia, we must *encourage* Missy to be independent of us! It is not her fault that God did not endow her with Alicia's looks, or my strength of character. And I began to see that a whole lifetime's exposure to my strength of character has not been good for Missy. I make the decisions about everything, and it is her nature to acquiesce without a fuss. So for far too long I have gone on making her decisions. I shall do so no longer."

"Rubbish!" snapped Octavia. "The girl's got no sense! Shoes instead of boots! Romances! Bush walks! It is my opinion that you must be more severe in future, not less."

Drusilla sighed. "When we were young women, Octavia, we wore shoes. Father was a very warm man, we lacked for nothing. We rode in carriages, we had plenty of pin-money. And ever since those days, no matter how hard life has been, at least you and I are able to look back and remember the pleasure of pretty shoes, pretty dresses, coming-out parties, *gaiety*. Where Missy has never worn a pair of pretty shoes, or a pretty dress. I'm not castigating myself for that, for it isn't my fault, but when I thought she might be going to die – well, I decided I was going to give her whatever she wanted, so long as I could afford it. Shoes I cannot afford, especially if there are going to be heavy doctor's bills. But if she wants to walk in the bush, or read romances – she may."

"Rubbish, rubbish, rubbish! You must go on as you have in the past. Missy needs strong direction."

And from that viewpoint Drusilla could not budge her.

Unaware of her mother's soul-searching, Missy decided she had better not read one of the new novels after dinner; she elected to tat instead.

"Aunt Octavia," she said, fingers flying, "how much lace do you plan to set into your new dress? Is this going to be enough, do you think? I can easily make you a lot more, but I'll need to know now."

Octavia held out her knobby hand and Missy deposited the bunched-up lace in it, leaving her aunt to spread out each piece on her lap.

"Oh, Missy, it is beautiful!" breathed Octavia, awed. "Drusilla, do look!"

Drusilla plucked a scrap out of her sister's lap and held it up to the weak light. "Yes, it is beautiful. You're improving all the time, Missy, I must say."

"Ah," said Missy gravely, "that is because I have finally learned to unknit the sleeve of ravelled care."

Both older ladies looked utterly blank for a moment, then Octavia cast a significant glance at Drusilla and ever so slightly shook her head. But Drusilla ignored her.

"Quite so," she said majestically.

Cutting a dash at Alicia's wedding won out; Octavia put Missy's brainstorm aside. "Is it enough lace, Drusilla?" she asked anxiously.

"Well, for what I had originally planned it's enough, but I've had a better idea. I'd like to let in some of the same lace all the way around the hem of the overskirt – *so* fashionable! Missy, would you mind doing so much extra work? Do be frank if you'd rather not."

Now Missy looked blank; in all her life her mother had never deferred to her before, nor stopped to think whether what she asked was excessive. Of course! It was the heart trouble! How amazing! "I don't mind in the least," she said quickly.

Octavia beamed. "Oh, thank you!" Her face puckered. "If only I might help you with the sewing, Drusilla. It's so much work for you."

Drusilla looked at the heap of lilac crêpe in her lap and sighed. "Don't worry, Octavia. Missy does all the fiddly bits like buttonholes and hems and plackets. But I do admit it would be wonderful to have a Singer sewing machine."

That of course was out of the question; the ladies of Missalonghi made their clothes the old-fashioned hard way, every inch of every seam sewn by hand. Drusilla did the main sewing and the cutting, Missy the fiddly bits; Octavia could not manage to hold an instrument so fine as a sewing needle.

"I am so very sorry your dress has to be brown, Missy," said Drusilla, and looked at her daughter pleadingly. "But it is lovely material, and it will make up very well, you wait and see. Would you like some beads on it?"

"And spoil the cut? Mother, you cut superbly, and the cut will carry it without any adornments," said Missy.

That night in bed Missy lay in the darkness and remembered the details of the loveliest afternoon of her entire life. For not only had he said hello to her, he had climbed down from his cart and actually chosen to walk along with her, chatting to her as if she was a friend rather than a mere member of that tiresome gang called Hurlingford. How nice he had looked. Homespun, but nice. And he smelled not of stale sweat, like so many of the oh-so-respectable Hurlingford men, but of sweet expensive soap; she had recognised it immediately because whenever the ladies of Missalonghi received rare gifts of such soap, it was not consumed upon their bodies (Sunlight was quite good enough for that!), but inserted between the folds of their clothes as they lay in drawers. And his hands might be toil-roughened, but they were clean, even beneath the nails. His hair too was immaculate; no trace of pomade or oil, just the healthy gloss one saw on the fur of a freshly licked cat. A prideful and scrupulous man, John Smith.

Best of all she liked his eyes, such a translucent golden brown, and so laughing. But she couldn't, *wouldn't* believe any of the tales hinting at dishonesty or baseness. Instead, she would have staked her life upon his intrinsic integrity and fiercely defended ethics. She could see such a man doing murder, perhaps, if goaded beyond endurance, but she could not see him stealing or cheating.

Oh, John Smith, I do love you! And I thank you from the very bottom of my heart for coming back to Missalonghi to see how I did.

With only a month left until her wedding, Alicia Marshall came day by day closer to the most perfect manifestation of her long and glorious blossoming, and she meant to enjoy even that final frantic month to the top of her bent. The date had been set eighteen months previously, and it had never occurred to her to doubt the season or the weather. Sure enough, though occasionally springs on the Blue Mountains might be late, or wet, or unduly windy, this one, obedient to Alicia's whim, was coming in with the halcyon dreaminess of Eden.

"It wouldn't dare do otherwise," said Aurelia to Drusilla, a nuance in her tone suggesting that just once Alicia's mother might enjoy Alicia's plans going awry.

Missy's Sydney appointment had been set up, but a week later than had been hoped; which was lucky for Missy, because on the Tuesday that Dr. Hurlingford had planned she should see the specialist, Alicia did not make her customary weekly trip to town. For on the Thursday of this week Alicia had scheduled her bridal party, and the preparations for it allowed of no other consideration, even hat shop business. The bridal party was not a humble sort of affair where modest kitchen gifts and girlish chatter prevailed; it was instead a formal reception for Alicia's female relatives of all ages, an occasion upon which everyone would have an opportunity to see and hear what would be expected of them on the Great Day. During the course of the festivities Alicia intended to announce the names of her bridesmaids, and show the designs and fabrics for the bridal party and the church décor.

The only blight came from Alicia's father and brothers, who brushed aside her attempts to enlist their help with a brusque impatience hitherto unknown.

"Oh, for God's sake, Alicia, go away!" snapped her father, more passion in his voice than she certainly could ever remember. "Have your wretched bridal party, by all means, but leave us out of it! There are times when women's affairs are a flaming nuisance, and this is one of them!"

"*Well*!" huffed Alicia, staylaces creaking dangerously, and went to complain to her mother.

"I'm afraid we must tread very carefully at the moment, dear," said Aurelia, looking worried.

"What on earth's the matter?"

"I don't really know, except that it's something to do with shares in the Byron Bottle Company. I gather they've been disappearing."

"Nonsense!" said Alicia. "Shares don't disappear."

"Out of the family? Is that what I mean?" amended Aurelia vaguely. "Oh, it's quite beyond me, I have no head for business."

"Willie hasn't mentioned it to me."

"Willie mightn't know yet, dear. He hasn't had much to do with the company yet, has he? After all, he's just finished at university."

Alicia dismissed the whole tiresome business with a snort, and went off to instruct the butler to the effect that only female servants would be allowed in the front of the house, as it was a party purely for ladies.

Of course Drusilla came, and brought Missy with her; poor Octavia, dying to go, was obliged at the last moment to remain behind in all her best clothes, as Aurelia had forgotten to arrange the promised conveyance for the ladies of Missalonghi. Drusilla wore her brown grosgrain, happy in the knowledge that to do so would not be exposing this tried-and-true outfit to an early encore at the wedding itself. And Missy wore her brown linen, on her head the old sailor hat she had been forced to don on every occasion demanding a hat for the last fifteen years, including church each Sunday. New hats would be forthcoming for the wedding, though not, alas, from Chez Chapeau Alicia; the basics were already bought from Uncle Herbert's emporium, and the final furbishings would be done at Missalonghi.

Alicia was looking stunning in a delicate apricot crêpe dress trimmed with lavender-blue embroidery and bearing a huge bunch of lavender-blue silk flowers on one shoulder. Oh, thought Missy, just this once I would love to be able to wear a dress like that! Now I *could* survive that apricot colour, I am positive I could! And I could survive that shade of blue too, it's halfway to pale purple.

Over a hundred women had been invited to the party. They wandered about the house in little clutches, catching sight of faces and catching up on gossip. Then at four o'clock they settled like roosting hens in the ballroom, where they partook of a magnificent tea of scones with jam and cream, petits fours, cucumber sandwiches, asparagus cornucopias, éclairs, cream buns and deliriously gooey Napoleons. There was even a choice between Darjeeling, Earl Grey, Lapsang Souchong and Jasmine tea!

Hurlingford women were traditionally fair, and traditionally tall, and traditionally incapable of frank speech. Looking around the gathering and listening to its chatter, Missy saw for herself the truth of these observations. This was the first occasion of its kind she had ever been invited to, probably because it would have been impolite not to invite her when so many women less closely related were coming. Somehow in church on Sunday the awesome presence of Hurlingford women en masse was watered down by the presence of a roughly equal number of Hurlingford men. But here in Aunt Aurelia's ballroom the breed was undiluted and overwhelming.

The air was thick with participles properly tucked away and exquisitely spliced infinitives and a great many other verbal delicacies largely gone out of fashion fifty years before. Under the splendour and graciousness of Aurelia's roof, no one dared to say "can't" or "won't" or "didn't". And, noted Missy, she herself was literally the only dark-haired woman there. Oh, a few borderline mouses glimmered (the greys and whites did not stand out at all), but her own jet-black hair was like a lump of coal in a field of snow; she quite understood why her mother had instructed her to keep her hat on throughout. Obviously, even when a Hurlingford man or woman married out of the family, he or she chose a blond partner. Indeed, Missy's own father had been very fair, but his grandfather, according to Drusilla, had been as dark as a dago, this term then being conventional and acceptable.

"Dearest Augusta and Antonia, it is the Saxon in us," fluted Drusilla to the sisters she saw least of.

Aurelia was devoting herself almost exclusively to Lady Billy, who had been amputated from her horse for the afternoon, not without bitter protest. And Lady Billy was sitting looking encephalitically expressionless, for she had no daughters of her own and no interest whatsoever in women. En masse they both frightened and upset her, and the greatest grief of her life had been the acquisition of Alicia Marshall as a prospective daughter-in-law. Undeterred by the fact that she fought a lone battle, Lady Billy had loudly opposed Little Willie's betrothal to his second cousin Alicia, declaring that they would never run together as a team, and would breed very poor stock. However, Sir William (called Billy) rode roughshod over her, as indeed he did over everybody; he had always had an eye for Alicia himself, and was delighted at the prospect of looking down his dining table every night to see Alicia's shining flaxen head and lovely face. For it had been arranged that the newlywed couple would reside at Hurlingford Lodge with Sir William and his lady for some months at least; Sir William's wedding present was prime land, ten acres of it, but the house built upon it was nowhere near finished.

Left very much to her own devices, Missy looked around for Una. She found Aunt Livilla, but no Una. How odd!

"I don't see Una here today," said Missy to Alicia when that ravishing creature drifted by with a bright and wonderfully condescending smile.

"Who?" asked Alicia, stopping.

"Una – Aunt Livilla's cousin – she works in the library."

"Silly girl, there's no Hurlingford by that name in Byron," said Alicia, who had never been known to read a book. And off she went to spread her glorious presence as thinly across the surface of the gathering as the layer of jam on a boarding school pudding.

At which point the penny dropped. Of course! Una was *divorced*! An unheard-of sin! Stirred to the extent of providing a roof over her cousin's head Aunt Livilla might have been, but her humanitarian instincts would never extend to allowing that cousin – that *divorced* cousin – to enter Byron society. So it seemed Aunt Livilla had decided to keep quiet about Una altogether. Come to think of it, Una herself had been the sole source of Missy's information;

on the rare occasions since Una's advent that Missy had found Aunt Livilla in the library, Aunt Livilla had never mentioned Una's name, and Missy, who was afraid of Aunt Livilla, had not mentioned Una either.

Drusilla bustled up, her sister Cornelia in tow. "Oh, is this not splendid?" she asked, speech patterns perfect.

"Very splendid," said Missy, shifting up on the sofa she had found behind a large potted Kentia palm cluster.

Drusilla and Cornelia sat down, replete with at least one specimen from every kind of delicacy offered at the buffet.

"So kind! So considerate! Dear Alicia!" waffled Cornelia, who regarded it as a great privilege to be permitted to work for a pittance as Alicia's sales dame, and had no idea how cynically Alicia traded on her gratitude and devotion. Until Chez Chapeau Alicia had opened its doors, Cornelia had worked for her brother Herbert in his alteration room, so there were grounds for her illusions; Herbert was so stingy he made Alicia look like a lady bountiful. In the same way as Octavia, and with the same result, Cornelia had sold her house and five acres to Herbert, only in her case it was to help her sister Julia pay her tea room off when Julia bought it from Herbert.

"Hush!" breathed Drusilla. "Alicia is going to speak."

Alicia spoke, cheeks glowing, eyes sparkling like bleached aquamarines. The names of the ten bridesmaids were greeted with squeals and claps; the chief bridesmaid fainted clean away from the honour of it, and had to be revived with smelling-salts. According to Alicia, the dresses for her attendants were to be paired in five shades of pink, from palest through to deep cyclamen, so that when the white-clad bride stood at the altar she would be flanked on either side by five attendants who gradually shaded from palest pink at the bride's end to rich dark pink at the farthest end.

"We are all very nearly the same height, all very fair, and of much the same figure," explained Alicia. "I think the effect will be remarkable."

"Is it not a brilliant concept?" whispered Cornelia, privileged to have been a party to the preliminary planning of the entire bridal. "Alicia's train will be of Alençon lace, twenty feet long, and cut on the full circle!"

"Magnificent," sighed Drusilla, remembering that the train on her own wedding gown had been of lace and even longer, but deciding not to say so.

"I notice Alicia has kept her choice to virgins only," said Missy, whose stitch had been bothering her ever since the seven-mile walk from Missalonghi, and now was growing worse. To leave the room was impossible, but nor could she sit still and silent a moment longer; to keep her mind off the pain, she started to talk. "Very orthodox of her," she continued, "but I'm *definitely* a virgin, and I didn't get picked."

"Sssssh!" hissed Drusilla.

"Dearest little Missy, you're too short and too dark," murmured Cornelia, feeling very sorry for her niece.

"I'm five feet seven in my stockinged feet," said Missy, making no effort to mute her voice. "Only among a collection of Hurlingfords would that be called short!"

"Sssssh!" hissed Drusilla again.

In the meantime Alicia had passed to the subject of flowers, and was informing her enthralled audience that every bouquet would consist of dozens of pink orchids that were coming down in chilled boxes on the Brisbane train.

"Orchids! How ostentatiously vulgar!" said Missy loudly.

"Sssssh!" from Drusilla, despairingly.

At this moment Alicia fell silent, having shot her bolt.

"You'd wonder that she's happy to give the whole show away at this early stage," said Missy to no one in particular, "but I suppose she thinks if she doesn't, half the details she's so proud of won't even be noticed."

Down swept Alicia upon them, laughing, glowing, her head full of limelight and her hands full of bridal sketches and swatches of fabric.

"It's such a pity you're so dark and so short, Missy," she said, very prettily. "I would have liked to ask you, but you must see that you wouldn't fit in as a bridesmaid."

"Well, I think it's a pity that *you're* not dark and short," said Missy, equally prettily. "With everyone around you of similar height and colouring, and all that gradual shading of pink, you're going to fade into the wallpaper."

Alicia gasped. Drusilla gasped. Cornelia gasped.

Missy got up in a leisurely manner and attempted to

shake the creases out of her brown linen skirt. "I think I'll be off now," she said chirpily. "Nice party, Alicia, but utterly undistinguished. Why does everybody have to serve the same old food? I would have appreciated a really good curried egg sandwich for a change."

She had gone before her audience managed to regain its breath; when it did, Drusilla was forced to hide a smile, and turn a deliberately deaf ear to Alicia's demand that Missy must be fetched back to apologise. Served Alicia right! Why couldn't she have been kind just this once, marred her perfect bridal group by including poor Missy in it? How amazing! Missy's analysis was spot on; Alicia *would* fade into the wallpaper, or rather into the pink and white bows and bouquets and bunting with which she intended to deck the church.

Just outside the front door of Mon Repos, the awful pain and airlessness struck. Deciding she would rather die in decent seclusion, Missy left the gravel drive and darted round the side of the house. Of course Aurelia Marshall's notions of garden layout did not permit a hint of thicket, so there were very few places wherein Missy might huddle undetected. The closest of these was a large clump of rhododendrons beneath one of the downstairs windows, so into the middle of the clump Missy crawled, and half-sat, half-lay with her back against the red brick behind the shrubs. The pain was unbearable, yet had to be borne. She closed her eyes and willed herself not to die until she could die in John Smith's arms, like the girl in *The Troubled Heart*. What a depressing place to be found all stiff and stark, Aunt Aurelia's rhododendron bushes!

She didn't die. After a little while the pain began to recede, and she began to stir. There were voices nearby, and, since the rhododendrons were still rather bare from their autumn pruning, she didn't want the talkers to come round the corner and find her. So she rolled over onto her knees and started to get up. That was when she realised that the voices were coming from the window just above her head.

"Did you ever see such a monstrosity of a hat?" asked a voice Missy recognised as belonging to Aunt Augusta's youngest daughter, Lavinia; of course Lavinia was a bridesmaid.

"All too often, in church every Sunday to be exact," said Alicia's tonelessly harsh voice. "Though I think the person underneath the hat is a far worse monstrosity."

"She's so *drab*!" came a third voice, belonging to the chief bridesmaid, Aunt Antonia's daughter Marcia. "Honestly, Alicia, you're according her far too much importance by calling her a monstrosity. Nonentity is a much better word for Missy Wright, though the hat, I grant you, is indeed a monstrosity."

"You have a point," conceded Alicia, who was still smarting from the unexpected flick of Missy's observation about fading into the wallpaper. Of course she was wrong! And yet Alicia knew that never again would the visual splendour of her wedding quite please her; Missy had planted her barb with more deadly skill than she realised.

"Do we really care about Missy Wright one way or another?" asked a more distant cousin called Portia.

"Due to the fact that her mother is my mother's favourite sister, Portia, I'm afraid I have to," declared Alicia in ringing tones. "Why Mama persists in pitying Auntie Drusie so, I don't know, but I've given up hoping I'll ever wean her from it. Oh, I daresay Mama's charity is laudable, but I can tell you that I try never to be at home on Saturday mornings, when Auntie Drusie comes to gorge herself on Mama's cakes. Lord, can she eat! Mama has Cook make two dozen fairy cakes, and by the time Auntie Drusie has gone, so have the fairy cakes, every last one." Alicia produced a brittle unamused laugh. "It's become a regular joke in our house, even among the servants."

"Well, they are dreadfully poor, aren't they?" asked Lavinia, who had been good at history at school, so aired her superiority by saying, "It always puzzled me why the French rabble guillotined Marie Antoinette, just because she said they should eat cake if they had no bread. It seems to me anyone dreadfully poor would adore the chance to eat cake for a change – I mean, look at Auntie Drusie!"

"Poor they are," said Alicia, "and poor I am afraid they are going to remain, with Missy their only hope."

That raised a general laugh.

"A pity one cannot have people condemned the way one

can have houses condemned," said another voice, a mere fourth or fifth cousin, by name of Junia; disappointment at not being chosen as a bridesmaid had concentrated all her natural venom down to one or two deadly drops.

"In this day and age, Junia, we are too kind for that," said Alicia. "Therefore we must all go on putting up with Auntie Drusie and Auntie Octie and Cousin Missy and Auntie Julie and Auntie Cornie and the rest of the spinster-widow brigade. Take my wedding. They will quite spoil it! But Mama rightly says they must be invited, and of course they will come the earliest and be the very last to go home. Haven't you noticed how pimples and boils always pop up when they're least welcome? However, Mama did have a brainwave that will spare us from those hideous brown dresses. She bought my household linens from Auntie Drusie for two hundred pounds. And I will admit that they do the most remarkably fine and dainty work, so Mama's money was not wasted, thank God. Embroidered pillow-slips closed with little covered buttons, and every last button embroidered with a tiny rosebud! Very beautiful! Anyway, Mama's scheme worked, because Uncle Herbert slipped the word to her that Missy came in and bought three dress-lengths – lilac for Auntie Drusie and blue for Auntie Octie. Any guesses what colour for Cousin Missy?"

"*Brown*!" chorused every voice, and then there was a gale of laughter.

"I have an idea!" cried Lavinia when the merriment

ceased. "Why don't you give Missy one of your own cast-offs in a shade that will suit her?"

"I'd rather be dead," said Alicia scornfully. "See one of my lovely dresses on that dago-looking scragbag? If you feel so strongly about it, my dear Lavinia, why don't you donate her one of your cast-offs?"

"I am not," said Lavinia tartly, "in your cosy financial position, Alicia, that's why! Think about it, since you're so peeved at her appearance. You wear a lot of amber and old gold and apricot. I imagine anything in that sort of range would look all right on Missy."

At which point Missy managed to get herself on hands and knees out of the rhododendrons and onto the path. She crept on all fours until she was well clear of the window, then got to her feet and ran. The tears were pouring down her face, but she wasn't about to stop and dry them, too angry and shamed to care who might see.

She hadn't thought anything anybody might say about her could hurt, for a thousand thousand times in her imagination she had catalogued the various pitying or contemptuous things that might conceivably be said about her. Nor did it hurt, really. What stabbed to the quick were the dreadful things Alicia and her friends had said about her mother and all those poor spinster aunts, so decent and honourable and hard-working, so grateful for any attention, yet so proud they would accept nothing they suspected might be charity. How dared Alicia speak of those infinitely more admirable women so scathingly, so unfeelingly! Let Alicia see how she would fare if she were placed in the same pinched shoes!

As she hurried through Byron with the stitch again burning in her side, Missy found herself praying that the library would be open, for Una would be in occupation. Oh, how she needed Una tonight! But the premises were dark, and a sign on the door simply said CLOSED.

Octavia was sitting in the kitchen of Missalonghi, changed back into her workaday clothes, with the small provender of their meal simmering away in a pot on the stove. Stew. Her misshapen hands were busy with knitting needles, magically producing the most fragile and cob-webby of evening shawls as a wedding present for the ungrateful Alicia.

"Ah!" she said, laying her task aside when Missy walked in. "Did you have a nice time, dear? Is your mother with you?"

"I had a wretched time, so I left ahead of Mother," said Missy briefly, then seized the milk bucket, and escaped.

The cow was waiting patiently to be let into the shed; Missy reached out to stroke the velvety dark muzzle, and looked deeply into the big sweet brown eyes.

"Buttercup, you're *much* nicer than Alicia, so I just don't understand why it's such an unforgivable insult to call a woman a cow. From now on, the women others call cows, I shall call Alicias," she told it as she led it into the shed, where it moved of its own accord into the milking stall. Buttercup was the easiest cow to milk, letting down without a struggle, never complaining if Missy's hands were cold, as they often were. Which of course was why its milk was so good; nice cows always gave nice milk.

Drusilla was home when Missy returned. It was customary to pour most of the milk into the big flat pans which lived on the shady side of the back verandah; as she poured, she could hear her mother enthusiastically regaling her aunt with a full description of Alicia's bridal party.

"Oh, I'm so glad one of you had a good time," said Octavia. "All I could get out of Missy was that she'd had a wretched time. I suppose her trouble is lack of friends."

"True, and no one is sorrier for it than I. But dear Eustace's death removed any chance of brothers and sisters for Missy, and this house is so far out of Byron on the wrong side that no one ever wants to come and see us regularly."

Missy waited for her sins to be divulged, but her mother made no reference to them. Courage seeping back, she went inside. Ever since the heart trouble came on it had become easier for her to assert herself, and apparently also easier for her mother to accept these signs of independence. Only it wasn't really the heart trouble that caused the change. It was Una. Yes, everything went back to Una's advent; Una's forthrightness, Una's frankness, Una's unwillingness to be sat on by anyone. Una would have told a supercilious twerp like James Hurlingford to go bite his bum, Una would have given Alicia something verbal to remember if she condescended, Una would always make sure people treated her with respect. And somehow this had rubbed off on such an unlikely pupil as Missy Wright.

When Missy walked in, Drusilla leaped up, beaming.

"Missy, you'll never guess!" she cried, reaching round to the back of the chair where she had been sitting and plucking a very large box off the floor. "As I was leaving the party, Alicia came and gave me this for you to wear at her wedding. She assured me that the colour would suit you beautifully, though I confess I would never have thought of it for myself. Only look!"

Missy stood turned to stone while her mother scrabbled in the box and unearthed a bundle of stiff and crushed organdie which she proceeded to shake out and hold up for Missy's dazed inspection. A gorgeous dress of a pale toffee shade, not tan and not yellow and not quite amber; those in the know would have understood that its frilled skirt and neckline put it at least five or six years out of date, but even so it was a gorgeous dress, and with extensive alterations it would suit Missy down to the ground.

"And the hat, only look at the hat!" squeaked Drusilla, clawing a huge cartwheel of pale toffee straw out of the box and twitching its artless piles of matching organdie into place. "Did you ever see a more beautiful hat? Oh, dearest Missy, you shall have a pair of shoes, no matter how impractical they are!"

The stone dropped away from Missy's limbs at last; she stepped forward, arms extended to receive Alicia's bounty, and her mother placed dress and hat in them at once.

"I'll wear my new brown satin and my home-made hat and good sturdy boots!" said Missy through her teeth, and took to her heels out the back door, the masses of organdie billowing up about her like the skirts on a swimming bêche-de-mer.

It was not yet fully dark; as she raced for the shed she could hear the frantic cries of her mother and aunt somewhere behind, but by the time they caught up with her, it was too late. The dress and hat were trampled beyond repair into the muck of the milking stall, and Missy, a shovel in her hands, was busy heaping every pile of dung she could find on top of Alicia's grand gesture.

Drusilla was unspeakably hurt. "How could you? Oh, how could you, Missy? Just this once in your life, you had a chance to look and feel like a belle!"

Missy laid the shovel against the shed wall and dusted her hands together in complete satisfaction. "You above all people ought to understand how I could, Mother," she said. "No one's pride is stiffer than yours, no one I know is quicker than you to interpret the most well-meaning gift as charity in disguise. Why then are you denying me my share of that pride? Would you have taken the gift for yourself? Why then take it for me? Do you honestly think Alicia did it to please me? Of course she didn't! Alicia is determined to have her wedding perfect down to the last guest, and I – I *spoiled* it! So she decided to make a silk purse out of Missy Wright the sow's ear. Well, thank you very much, but I'd rather be my own sow's ear in all its natural homeliness than any silk purse of Alicia's making! And so I shall tell her!"

And so indeed she did tell her, the very next day. Though Drusilla had crept out in the dead of night armed with a lamp, the dress and hat had disappeared from their vile resting place, and she never saw them again; nor did she ever discover what had happened to them, for no one who knew remembered to tell her, so shocking were the other events of that memorable Friday morning in the Marshall residence.

Missy arrived at the front door of Mon Repos about ten o'clock, hampered by a large and exceedingly well wrapped parcel which she carried rather gingerly by a string loop. Had the butler any idea of the consternation already reigning in the small drawing room, it is doubtful whether Missy would have got any further than the front stoop, but luckily the butler did not have any idea, and so was able to contribute his mite to the general atmosphere of disaster.

The small drawing room, not really small, was nonetheless rather full of very large people when Missy sidled round the door with her parcel on its string. Aunt Aurelia was there, and Uncle Edmund, and Alicia, and Ted and Randolph, and the third Sir William, and his son and heir, Little Willie;

Lady Billy was not there, as she was assisting a mare to foal.

"I don't understand it!" Edmund Marshall was saying as Missy gave the butler a smile and a gesture which indicated she would announce herself as soon as maybe. "I just don't understand it! How could so many shares escape us? *How?* And who the hell sold them and who the hell bought them?"

"As far as my agents can gather," said the third Sir William, "every share not held by a Hurlingford proper was bought up for many times its actual value, and then the mystery buyer began to make inroads on shares held by Hurlingfords. How or when or why I don't know, but he managed to discover every Hurlingford in need of money and every Hurlingford not tied to Byron, and he made offers no one could refuse."

"It's ridiculous!" cried Ted. "For the sort of money he's been paying, there's absolutely no way he can ever recoup his outlay. I mean, the Byron Bottle Company is a very nice little enterprise, but it's not gold we're taking out of the ground, nor is it the elixir of life! Yet the prices he's been paying are the sort of prices a speculator might pay on receipt of an infallible tip that the ground is solid gold."

"I agree with all that," said Sir William, "but I can't give you an answer, because I just don't know it."

"Are we reduced to minority shareholders, Uncle Billy, is that what you're trying to say?" asked Alicia, who was fully acquainted with the practices and terminology of the business world – and a not inconsiderable shareholder in the Byron Bottle Company herself, since Chez Chapeau Alicia had put capital in her hands and an acquisitive nature had tempted her into the safer realms of speculation.

"Good God, no, not yet!" cried Sir William; then, with less confidence, he added, "However, I admit it's going to be touch and go unless we can either stem the tide of shares we're losing, or buy more ourselves."

"Aren't there any stray small shareholders living here in Byron whom we can get to first?" asked Randolph.

"A few, Hurlingfords on the distaff side mostly, and two or three of the old maids who accidentally inherited shares they weren't really entitled to. Naturally they've never been paid a dividend."

"How did you manage that, Uncle Billy?" asked Randolph.

Sir William snorted. "What do they know about shares, silly old biddies like Cornelia and Julia and Octavia? I didn't want them thinking they were hanging onto something valuable, so as well as never paying them a dividend, I told them the shares were worthless because they belonged by rights to Maxwell and Herbert. However, rather than make a big fuss, I merely told them they could best rectify the mistake by willing the shares to the sons of Maxwell and Herbert."

"Clever!" said Alicia admiringly.

Sir William gave her one of his hot lusting glances; she was beginning to wonder privately how easy it was going to be to keep Uncle Billy at arm's length after she married and

100

moved into Hurlingford Lodge – but cross that bridge later.

"We'll have to acquire the old maids' shares now," said Edmund Marshall, looking very gloomy. "Though, Billy, I must be frank and admit that I don't know how I'm going to find any ready money. I'd have to retrench drastically, which would be most disagreeable for my family – Alicia's wedding, you know."

"I'm in the same boat myself, old man," said Sir William, the words sticking in his gullet. "It's all this flap over a big war in Europe, dammit! Rumour-mongering is all!"

"Why *buy* the shares?" asked Alicia, just the smallest tinge of contempt for their stupidity in her voice. "All you have to do is go to Auntie Cornie and Auntie Julie and Auntie Octie and *ask*! They'll hand them over without a murmur!"

"All right, we can do that with those three, and with Drusilla as well, I imagine. What on earth possessed Malcolm Hurlingford to leave shares to his daughters, I ask you? He always was soft over his girls, though thank God Maxwell and Herbert don't take after their father in that regard." Sir William sighed impatiently. "A pretty pickle we're in! Even if, as Alicia says, the old biddies hand over their shares without a murmur, we've still got to deal with the various ne'er-do-wells and half-Hurlingfords who most certainly won't want to part with what shares they have for nothing. Oh, we'll manage, I have no doubt, just as long as they don't get wind of the mystery buyer. Because we can't match his prices."

"What can we sell in a hurry to raise cash?" asked Alicia crisply.

They all turned to look at her, and Missy, as yet quite unnoticed, shifted stealthily from her spot in front of the door (against which her brown dress and person didn't show at all) to a safer spot behind one of the potted Kentia palms Aunt Aurelia had placed everywhere inside her lovely house.

"There's Lady Billy's bloody horses, for a start," said Sir William with relish.

"My jewels," said Aurelia with great resolution.

"And my jewels," said Alicia with a nasty look at her mother for getting in first.

"The thing is," said Edmund, "that this mystery buyer, whoever he – or they – might be, seems to know more about who owns shares in the Byron Bottle Company than we do, and we're the board of directors! When I consulted our list of shareholders I discovered that in a great many cases the shares had passed from the person listed as owning them into other hands, mostly sons or nephews, admittedly, but strange hands nonetheless. It never occurred to me that *any* Hurlingford would sign away his birthright this side of death!"

"Times are changing," sighed Aurelia. "When I was a girl, Hurlingford clannishness was a legend. Nowadays it seems as if some of the young Hurlingfords don't give a tuppenny bumper about the family."

"They've been spoiled," said Sir William. He cleared his throat, slapped his hands on his thighs, and said with great decision, "All right, I suggest we leave matters as they stand over the weekend, then on Monday we get down to raising some cold hard cash."

"Who is to approach the aunties?" asked Ted.

"Alicia," said Sir William instantly. "Only not until a bit closer to her wedding, I think. That way she can hoodwink them into thinking they're giving her a wedding present."

"Won't the mystery buyer get to them first?" asked Ted, who always worried about everything, and so had drifted into accounting quite naturally.

"One thing you can be absolutely sure of, Ted, is that none of those silly old chooks would dream of parting with anything Hurlingford to anyone outside the family without first asking me or Herbert. The buyer could offer them a fortune, and they'd still insist upon consulting me or Herbert first." So positive was Sir William of his ground on this point that he smiled when he said it.

Taking advantage of the general mêlée as several worried and overwrought people endeavoured to find the right way to break off their meeting, Missy slid out the door and came back inside very noisily. And they all noticed her at once, though none of them looked pleased to see her.

"What do you want?" asked Alicia rudely.

"I came to show you how I feel about your charity, Alicia, and to tell you that I am happy to come to your wedding in good old brown," said Missy, marching across the room and dumping her parcel on the table in front of Alicia. "There! Thank you, but no thank you."

Alicia stared at her much as she might have stared at a dog turd she had almost stepped in. "Please yourself!"

"I intend to, from now on." She glanced up at the much taller Alicia (who admitted to five feet ten but was actually six feet one) with a puckish grin. "Go on, Alicia, open it! I dyed it brown just for you."

"You what?" Alicia began to fumble with the knots in the string, so Randolph came to her rescue with his pocket knife. After the string was cut the wrapping parted easily, and there lay the beautiful organdie dress and the ravishing hat, unspeakably smirched with what looked – and smelled – like fresh, sloppy, healthy cow and pig dung.

Alicia let out a squeak of horror that kept on growing and swelling until it became a long thin screech, and jumped away from the table as her mother, father, brothers, uncle and fiancé crowded round to see.

"You – you disgusting little trollop!" she snarled at the beaming Missy.

"Oh, I am not!" said Missy smugly.

"You're worse than a trollop! And you may count yourself lucky indeed that I am too much of a lady to tell you exactly what I do think you are!" gasped Alicia, hardly knowing which had shocked her most, the deed, or the doer of the deed.

"Then you may count yourself unlucky that I am not too much of a lady to tell you exactly what I think you are, Alicia. I am only three days older than you, which puts you a lot closer to thirty-four than it does to thirty-three. Yet, here you are, mutton dressed up as lamb, brazen as brass, about to marry a boy hardly more than *half* your age! His father's years are more suitable! And that makes you a cold-blooded cradle-snatcher! When Montgomery Massey died before you could haul him to the altar – thereby escaping a fate worse than death – you couldn't see anyone on your horizon who was a tenth as good a catch. And then you spied poor Little Willie, still with all his baby-curls, playing with his hoop in his sailor suit, and you decided to be Lady Willie one day. I have no doubt that had the circumstances changed, you'd have been just as happy to be Lady Billy instead of Lady Willie – happier maybe, since the title's already there. I admire your gall, Alicia, but I do not admire you. And I feel very sorry for poor Little Willie, who is going to lead a wretched life, a bone between his wife and his mother."

The object of her pity was standing, with the rest of his relatives, gaping at Missy as if she had jumped stark naked out of a gigantic cake and proceeded to do the can-can. Aurelia had mercifully gone into hysterics, but so mesmerised was the rest of Missy's audience that it had failed to notice the fact.

Sir William recovered first. "Get out of this house!"

"I'm on my way," said Missy, looking very pleased.

"I will never forgive you for this!" cried Alicia. "How dare you? How *dare* you?"

"Oh, go bite your bum!" said Missy, and laughed. "It's big enough," she added, and departed.

This was the proverbial last straw; Alicia stiffened until she became utterly rigid, gave a gurgling moaning shriek, and fell over with a crash to join her mother on the floor.

Oh, how *satisfying* that had been! But as she walked away down the gradual hill of George Street that led into the main thoroughfare of Byron, Missy's elation faded. Compared to the topic under discussion during her first and unnoticed tenure of the drawing room, the presentation of Alicia's violated clothing was picayune. Those poor women! Missy knew as little about the world of company business as her mother and aunts, but she was fully intelligent enough to have caught the drift of Sir William's words. She even knew of the shares, for Drusilla kept hers and Octavia's both in the small tin cash-box that lay inside her wardrobe and held things like the deeds to her house and five acres of land. Ten shares each, twenty shares altogether. Which meant that Aunt Cornelia and Aunt Julia probably had ten shares each as well. Dividend. That was obviously some sort of periodic payment, a share in the company's profits.

How very despicable most of her male relations were! Sir William, eager to keep that disgraceful policy of the first Sir William's going, so that the hapless female members of his family who pinched and scraped in grinding but genteel poverty should have none of the fruits that accrued from the bottling of what was, after all, in God's gift rather than in any Hurlingford's. Uncle Maxwell, who was the worst kind of thief, rich in his own right, yet stealing the eggs and butter and orchardings of his poor relations because he had bullied them into believing that to sell elsewhere would be an unforgivable act of disloyalty. Uncle Herbert, who had bought up many of those houses on five acres in his time, always for a great deal less than they were worth, being the same kind of bully as his brother Maxwell. Only he was worse, because he stole back the little he paid out as well, by telling his victims that the investment schemes designed to make that little a little more had failed.

Not only the male relations were despicable, Missy amended, in a mood to dish out criticisms fairly. If the Aurelias and Augustas and Antonias had brought pressure to bear, having married on the inside of the clan fortunes, maybe they might have succeeded in changing things, for the worst bully is vulnerable to being bullied by his wife.

Well, something must be done. But what? Missy debated carrying her tale home, then decided she would not be believed, or if believed, that her mother and aunts would still end in being bullied out of their just due. Something *had* to be done, and done soon, before Alicia came smarming round to secure the shares, as secure them she undoubtedly would.

The library was open today; Missy glanced through the window expecting to see Aunt Livilla's grim form behind the desk, but there instead was Una. So she slowed down, turned round, and backtracked.

"Missy! What a treat! I didn't expect to see you today, darling," said Una, smiling as if she really did think it a treat to see the family trollop cum scragbag.

"I'm so angry!" cried Missy, and sat down on the hard chair provided for browsers, fanning herself with her hand.

"What's the matter?"

Suddenly realising she couldn't possibly expose that small clutch of close blood-relations to the contempt of a person as remotely connected to the Byron arm of the clan as Una, she had to compromise with a lame, "Oh, nothing."

Una didn't attempt to probe. She just nodded and smiled, that lovely radiance emanating from skin and hair and nails subtly soothing rage.

"How about a cup of tea before the long hike home?" she asked, getting up.

A cup of tea assumed the proportions of a life-giving elixir; "Yes, please!" said Missy with fervour.

Una disappeared behind the last bookshelf at the back of the room, where in a small cubicle there lay facilities for making tea; there was no toilet, the norm in Byron shops, for everyone was expected to use the toilets in the Byron Waters Baths, and be quick about it.

To investigate the novels while she waited seemed like a

good idea to Missy, so she moved to the back of the room and inched along the shelf that came hard up against the edge of Aunt Livilla's desk. And her eye in moving sideways round the desk to where the shelf continued on its far side encountered a familiar-looking sheaf of papers lying there. A packet of share certificates in the Byron Bottle Company.

Una emerged. "Kettle's on, but it takes time to boil from scratch on a spirit stove." Her eyes followed Missy's, then came to rest on Missy's face. "Isn't it lovely?" she asked.

"What?"

"The money that's being offered for Byron Bottle Company shares, of course. Ten pounds a pop! Unheard of! Wallace had a few shares of mine, you know, and when we separated he gave them back to me – said he didn't want anything that reminded him of the Hurlingfords. I only have ten shares, but I can definitely use a hundred quid at the moment, darling. And just between you and me, Auntie Livvie is a bit on the short side too, so I've persuaded her to give me her twenty shares to sell while I'm selling mine."

"How did Aunt Livilla manage to acquire shares?"

"Richard gave them to her when he couldn't pay her back in cash the time he needed money so desperately he actually borrowed from her. Poor Richard! He never can bet on the right horses. And she's such a stickler for repayment of loans, even when it's her only beloved son on the borrowing end. So he signed over a few of his shares in the Byron Bottle Company to her, and that shut her up."

"Has he got more?"

"Naturally. He's a male Hurlingford, darling. But I do believe he may have sold out completely, because it was Richard put me onto this godsend of a buyer."

"How can you sell someone else's shares?"

"With a Power of Attorney. See?" Una held up a stiff foolscap form. "You get it at the stationer's, like a will form. And you fill it out with the details, and you sign it, and whoever is giving you permission to act on her behalf signs it, and someone signs it as a witness."

"I see," said Missy, forgetting all about perusing the novels. She sat down again. "Una, do you have an address for whoever is buying Byron Bottle shares?"

"Right here, darling, though I'm taking the whole kit and kaboodle down to Sydney in person on Monday to sell them, it's safer. That's why I'm minding the library today, so I can have Monday off." She got up and went back to make the tea.

Missy thought hard. Why couldn't she, Missy, have a try at getting hold of the aunts' certificates before Alicia came asking for them? Why should Alicia fill her with defeat when in their sole clash just concluded, Alicia had been the loser?

By the time Una came back with the tea tray, Missy had made up her mind.

"Oh, thank you." She took her cup gratefully. "Una, is it imperative that you go to Sydney on Monday? Could you possibly make it Tuesday instead?"

"I don't see why not."

"I have an appointment with a Macquarie Street specialist next Tuesday morning," Missy explained carefully. "I was going with Alicia, but... I don't think she's going to want my company, somehow. It's possible I may have some of these shares to sell, and if I could go with you, it would be easier. I've only been to Sydney a couple of times when I was a child, so I don't know the place."

"Oh, what fun! Tuesday it is." Una fairly glittered, so bright had the light in her become.

"I'll have to ask you for another favour, I'm afraid."

"Of course, darling. What?"

"Would you mind going next door to the stationer's and buying me four of these Power of Attorney forms? You see, if I go myself, Uncle Septimus is sure to want to know what I need Power of Attorney forms for, and the next thing he'll mention it to Uncle Billy, or Uncle Maxwell, or Uncle Herbert, and – well, I'd rather keep my business to myself."

"I'll go the minute I finish my cup of tea, while you're here to mind the shop for me."

And so it was arranged, including Una's driving out to Missalonghi on Sunday afternoon at five o'clock to witness the signing of the forms. Luckily this time Missy had her own little money-purse with her, and luckily it contained two shillings; the forms were expensive, at threepence each.

"Thank you," said Missy, stowing the rolled-up forms in her shopping bag.

She had decided upon some books as well.

"Good lord!" exclaimed Una, glancing at the titles. "Are you sure you want *The Troubled Heart*? I thought you said you read it to death all last week."

"I did. But I still want to read it again." And into the bag alongside the forms went *The Troubled Heart*.

"I'll see you at Missalonghi on Sunday afternoon, and don't worry, Auntie Livvie never minds lending me her horse and sulky," said Una, accompanying Missy to the door, where she deposited a light kiss on Missy's unaccustomed cheek. "Chin up, girl, you can do it," she said, and pushed Missy out into the street.

"Mother," said Missy that evening as she sat in the warmth of the kitchen with Drusilla and Octavia, "have you still got those Byron Bottle shares Grandfather left you and Aunt Octavia in his will?"

Drusilla looked up from her beading warily; though the altered pecking-order was of her own making, she still found it a little difficult to accept the fact that she was no longer the boss-chook. And she had learned very quickly to spot the more subtle, oblique approach Missy employed, so that she knew something was in the wind now.

"Yes, I've still got them," she said.

Missy put her tatting in her lap and looked across at her mother very seriously. "Mother, do you trust me?"

Drusilla blinked. "Of course I do!"

"How much is a new Singer sewing machine?"

"I don't honestly know, but I imagine at least twenty or thirty pounds, perhaps a great deal more."

"If you had yet another hundred pounds besides the two hundred pounds Aunt Aurelia paid for Alicia's linens, would you buy yourself a Singer sewing machine?"

"I would certainly be tempted."

"Then give me your shares in Byron Bottle and let me sell them for you. I can get you ten pounds a share in Sydney."

Both Drusilla and Octavia had ceased working.

"Missy dear, they're worthless," said Octavia gently.

"No, they are not worthless," said Missy. "You've been duped by Uncle Billy and Uncle Herbert and the rest, is all. You should have been paid what's called a dividend upon them every so often, because the Byron Bottle Company is an extremely prosperous concern."

"No, you're wrong!" insisted Octavia, shaking her head.

"I'm right. If you two and Aunt Cornelia and Aunt Julia had only taken yourselves off to a disinterested solicitor in Sydney years ago, you might be a lot richer today than you are, and that's the truth."

"We could never go behind the menfolk's back, Missy," said Octavia. "It would be a breach of faith and trust in them. They know better than we do, which is why they look after us and watch out for us. And they're *family*!"

"Don't I know it?" cried Missy from behind clenched teeth. "Aunt Octavia, your menfolk have been trading on the fact that they're family ever since the Hurlingfords began! They *use* you! They exploit you! When have we ever got a fair price from Uncle Maxwell for our produce? Do you honestly swallow all those hard-luck stories of his about being done down in the markets himself, so how can he afford to pay us more? He's as rich as Croesus! And when have you ever seen proof that Uncle Herbert actually did lose your money in an unlucky investment? He's richer than Croesus! And didn't Uncle Billy tell you in person that those shares were worthless?"

The fixity of Drusilla's silent regard had passed from shock to doubt, from unwillingness to listen to a distinct desire to hear more. And by the end of this impassioned speech, even Octavia was visibly wavering. Perhaps had it been the old Missy sitting there destroying the old order, they might have dismissed what she said without a qualm; but this new Missy possessed an authority which lent her words the ring of unequivocal truth.

"Look," Missy went on more quietly, "I can sell your shares in the Byron Bottle Company for ten pounds each, and I know that kind of opportunity is as rare as hen's teeth, because I was there when Uncle Billy and Uncle Edmund were talking about it, and that's what they said. They didn't know I was listening, otherwise they'd not have said a word of it. They spoke of you as they think of you, with utter contempt. Believe me, I did not misinterpret what I heard, and I do not exaggerate. And I made up my mind that there was going to be an end to it, that I was going to see that you and Aunt Cornelia and Aunt Julia got the better of them for once. So give me your shares and let me sell them for you, because I'll get you ten pounds each for them. But if you offer them to Uncle Billy or Uncle Herbert or Uncle Maxwell, they'll bully you into signing them away for nothing."

Drusilla sighed. "I wish I didn't believe you, Missy, but I do. And what you say comes as no surprise, deep down."

Octavia, who might have battled on in blind loyalty, instead decided to switch allegiances; for she was a little bit of a child, and craved firm direction.

"Think what a difference a Singer sewing machine would make to you, Drusilla," she said.

"I would enjoy it," admitted Drusilla.

"And I must confess I would enjoy having a hundred pounds all of my own in the bank. I would feel less of a burden."

Drusilla capitulated. "Very well, then, Missy, you may have our shares to sell."

"I want Aunt Cornelia's and Aunt Julia's as well!"

"I see."

"I can sell their shares for the same amount of money, ten pounds each. But like you, they must be prepared to give me their shares without one word to Uncle Billy or any of the others – not one word!"

"Cornelia could certainly do with the money, Drusilla," said Octavia, feeling more cheerful every moment, and consigning her male relatives to limbo because it was better to do that than grieve over their perfidy, bleed from their hurtfulness. "She could afford to have her feet done by that German bone specialist in Sydney. She does so much standing! And you know how desperate Julia's case is, now that the Olympus Café has put in that extra room out the back, with marble-topped tables and a pianist every afternoon. If she had an extra hundred pounds, she could afford to make her tea room even swankier than the Olympus Café."

"I'll do my best to talk them into it," said Drusilla.

"Well, if you do talk them into it, they have to be here at Missalonghi on Sunday afternoon at five o'clock, with their shares. All of you will have to sign a Power of Attorney."

"What's that?"

"A piece of paper that authorises me to act in your name."

"Why at five o'clock on Sunday?" asked Octavia.

"Because that's when my friend Una is coming to witness the signing of the documents."

"Oh, how nice!" Inspiration struck Octavia. "I shall bake her a batch of my plain biscuits."

Missy grinned. "For once in our lives, Aunt Octavia, I think we can treat ourselves to a slap-up Sunday high tea. We can have plain biscuits for Una, of course, but we'll have fairy cakes and melting moments and cream puffs iced with toffee, and – *lamingtons*!"

No one gave her any argument about that menu.

*

When Missy arrived at the Byron railway station at six o'clock on Tuesday morning, she carried forty shares in the Byron Bottle Company, and four duly signed and witnessed Powers of Attorney. Una, it turned out, was a proper Justice of the Peace in spite of her sex (she said it happened in Sydney from time to time), and had fixed a most official-looking seal to the documents.

She was waiting on the platform, and so was Alicia. Not together, for Alicia was at the engine end, where the first class carriages would stand, and Una was at the guard's van end, where the second class carriages would stand.

"I hope you don't mind travelling second class," said Missy anxiously. "Mother has been most generous, I have ten shillings for my expenses and a guinea for the specialist, but I don't want to spend any more of it than I can help."

"Darling, my first class days are long over," soothed Una. "Besides, it's not a terribly long journey, and at this time of a cold morning, no one is going to insist that the windows be opened to let in the soot."

Missy's eyes encountered Alicia's; Alicia sniffed and deliberately turned the other way. Thank heavens for that, thought Missy unrepentantly.

The rails began to hum, and shortly afterwards the train came in, a huge black monster of an engine with a stubby stack clunking past in torrents of grimy smoke and fierce gushes of thick white steam.

"Do you know what I like to do?" asked Una of Missy

as they found themselves a couple of vacant seats, one a window.

"No, what?"

"You know the overhead bridge at the bit of Noel Street near the bottling plant?"

"I do indeed."

"I love to stand right in the middle on top of it, and hang over the edge of the parapet when a train goes underneath. Whoosh! Smoke everywhere, just like descending to hell. But oh, such fun!"

And so are you fun, thought Missy. I've never met anyone like you, nor anyone so full of life.

By the time the train drew into its terminus at Central Station, the hands of the platform clock said twenty minutes to nine. Her appointment in Macquarie Street was for ten, but Una said that left them plenty of time for a cup of tea in the railway refreshment rooms. Alicia swept by them in the main concourse; she must have been lurking in wait just to do it, for the first class passengers were normally well ahead of those at the back of the train.

"Isn't that the famous Alicia Marshall?" asked Una.

"Yes."

Una made an untranslatable sound.

"What do you think of her?" asked Missy, curious.

"Obvious and flashy, darling. Keeps all her goods in the shop window, and you know what happens to goods in shop windows, don't you?"

"I do, but tell me in your own words."

Una giggled. "Darling, they *fade*! Constant exposure to the glaring light of day. I give her another year at most. After that, no amount of lacing her stays tighter will keep her figure trim. She'll grow enormously fat and lazy, and she'll develop the most dreadful temper. I believe she's going to marry a mere lad. Pity. What she needs is a man who will make her work very hard, and treat her like dirt."

"Poor Little Willie is too limp, I fear," sighed Missy, and had no idea why Una found that remark so exquisitely funny.

In fact, Una laughed in fits and starts all the way down Castlereagh Street on the tram, but she refused to tell Missy why, and by the time they reached the building on Macquarie Street where the specialist had his rooms, Missy had given up.

At ten on the dot, Dr. George Parkinson's haughty nurse took her into a room plentifully endowed with movable screens of terrifying cleanliness and whiteness. She was directed to remove all her clothes, including her bloomers, place an indicated white wrap around her scrawny person, and lie down on the couch to wait for Doctor.

What an odd way to meet anyone, she couldn't help thinking when Dr. Parkinson's face loomed over hers; she was left to wonder what he looked like when the hairy caverns of his nostrils were not his most prominent feature. With his nurse in silent attendance, he thumped her chest, stared at her pitifully under-developed breasts with the rudeness of utter indifference, listened to her heart and lungs through a far sleeker stethoscope than Dr. Hurlingford's, took her pulse, stuck a spatula down her throat until she gagged dangerously, felt both sides of her neck and under her chin with impatient hard fingers, then went rolling round her flinching belly with his palms.

"Internal examination, Nurse," he said curtly.

"Pee ar or pee vee?" asked Nurse.

"Both."

The internal examinations left Missy feeling as if she had undergone some sort of major operation without benefit of chloroform, but there was worse to come. Dr. Parkinson flipped her over onto her front and then went poking and prying along the cordillera of her backbone until, somewhere around the spot where her shoulder blades stuck out like pathetic wings, he grunted several times.

"Ahah!" he exclaimed, striking treasure-trove.

Without any warning, Missy was grabbed around head and heels and hips by doctor and nurse combined; what they did was over so quickly she had no positive idea what they did, except that there came the sound of a grinding, sickening crunch all the more horrifying because she heard it inside her ears as well as outside them.

"You may get dressed now, Miss Wright, and then go through that door," ordered Dr. Parkinson, and went through that door himself with his nurse still in attendance.

Shaken and diminished, Missy did as she was told.

The right way up he turned out to have a very pleasant face, and his light blue eyes were kind and interested.

"Well, Miss Wright, you may return home today," he said, fingering a letter that lay on his desk along with quite a number of other papers.

"Am I all right?" asked Missy.

"Perfectly all right. There's absolutely nothing wrong with your heart. You've got a badly pinched nerve near the top of your spine, and those vigorous walks of yours kinked it into a vigorous protest, that's all."

"But – I couldn't breathe!" whispered Missy, aghast.

"Panic, Miss Wright, panic! When the nerve kinks the pain is very severe, and it is just possible that in your case it inhibits some of the respiratory musculature. But there's really no need to worry. I manipulated your spine myself now, and that should fix it up as long as you slow down the pace of your walking a little when you're going some distance. If it doesn't clear up, I suggest you rig yourself up a sort of chinning bar, have someone tie a couple of house-bricks to each of your feet, and then try to lift yourself up to your chin on the bar against the weight of the bricks."

"And there's nothing else wrong with me?"

"Disappointed, eh?" asked Dr. Parkinson shrewdly. "Come now, Miss Wright! Why on earth would you prefer to have heart trouble instead of a kinked spinal nerve?"

It was a question Missy had no intention of answering

aloud; how could one die in John Smith's arms of a kinked spinal nerve? It was as romantic as pimples.

Dr. Parkinson sat back in his chair and regarded her thoughtfully, tapping his pen on the blotter. It was obviously his habit to do this, for the blotter was pocked with many little blue dots, and at times, perhaps from boredom, he had begun to join up the more scattered dots into a meaningless cat's cradle.

"Periods!" he said suddenly, apparently feeling he ought to cheer her up a little by investigating every avenue. "How often do you have a period, Miss Wright?"

She blushed, and hated herself for blushing. "About every six months."

"Lose much?"

"No, very little."

"Pain? Cramps?"

"No."

"Hmmmm." He began to join up some dots. "Head-aches?"

"No."

"Are you a fainter?"

"No."

"Hmmmm." He pursed his lips so successfully that the top one actually managed to caress the tip of his nose. "Miss Wright," he said at last, "what really ails you can only be effectively cured if you find yourself a husband and have a couple of babies. I doubt you'd ever have more than a couple, because I don't think you'll fall easily, but at your age it's high time you got started."

"If I could find someone willing to start me, Doctor, believe me I would start!" said Missy tartly.

"I beg your pardon."

At this precise and uncomfortable moment Dr. Parkinson's nurse thrust her head around the door and wiggled her brows.

He rose immediately, semaphored away. "Excuse me."

For perhaps a minute Missy sat immobile in her chair wondering whether she ought to get up and tiptoe out, then she decided she had better wait for a formal dismissal. Dr. Neville Hurlingford's name leaped at her from the top of a letter on the desk, midway between a constellation of joined dots and a globular cluster of unjoined dots. Quite independently of her brain, Missy's hand reached out, picked up the letter.

"Dear George," it said,

"Odd that I should have to send you two patients within the same week, when I haven't sent you any in six months. But such is life – and my practice – in Byron. This letter is to introduce Missy Wright, a poor little old maid who has had at least one attack of chest pain and breathlessness following on a long, brisk walk. The single attack witnessed was rather suggestive of hysteria except that the patient was grey and sweating. However, her return to normal was dramatically sudden, and when I examined her not long afterwards, I could find no sequelae of any kind. I do indeed suspect hysteria, as her life's circumstances would make it a most likely diagnosis. She leads a stagnant, deprived existence (vide her breast development). But to be on the safe side, I would like you to see her with a view to excluding any serious illness."

Missy put the letter down and closed her eyes. Did the whole world see her with pity and contempt? And how could pride contend with so much pity and contempt when it was so well-meaning? Like her mother, Missy was proud. "Stagnant". "Deprived". "A poor little old maid". "With a view to excluding any serious illness", as if stagnation and deprivation and old maidenhood were not serious illnesses within themselves!

She opened her eyes, surprised to discover that they contained not one tear. Instead, they were bright and dry and *angry*. And they began searching through the litter on Dr. Parkinson's desk to see if among the pieces of paper there might be at least the start of a report on her condition. She found two reports, neither distinguished by a name; one had a list of findings on it that all said "normal", the other was a technical litany of disaster, all to do with the heart. And she discovered the beginning of a letter to Dr. Hurlingford.

"Dear Neville," the letter said,

"Thank you for referring Mrs. Anastasia Gilroy and Miss ? Wright, whose Christian name I am afraid I do not know, as everyone including yourself seems to add a 'y' to her marital status and leave it at that. I am sure you will not object if I send you my opinion about both patients in this one" –

And there it ended. Mrs. Anastasia Gilroy? After sifting through a few of the non-Hurlingford faces in Byron, she came up with a sickly-looking woman of about her own age who lived in a rundown cottage beside the bottling plant with a drunken husband and several small, neglected children.

Was the second clinical report about Mrs. Gilroy, then? Missy picked it up and tried to decipher the jargon and symbols which filled the top half of the sheet. Though the bottom half was clear enough, even to her.

It said, "I can offer no course of treatment able to change or modify this prognosis. The patient is suffering from an advanced form of multiple valvular disease of the heart. If no further cardiac deterioration takes place, I give her six months to one year of life. However, I can see no point in recommending bed rest, as I imagine this patient would simply ignore the directive, given her nature and home situation."

Mrs. Gilroy? If only there was a name on it! But it would be hers, saved to put in with the letter to Dr. Hurlingford. There were no other reports amid the confusion. Oh, why wasn't Missy Wright's the bad report? Death, snatched from her, seemed suddenly very sweet and desirable. It wasn't fair! Mrs. Gilroy had a family who needed her desperately. Where Missy Wright had no one to need her desperately.

Voices sounded on the other side of the door; Missy folded up the report still in her hand neatly and swiftly, and stuffed it into her purse.

"My dear Miss Wright, I am so sorry!" cried Dr. Parkinson, breezing in with sufficient flurry to send the papers on his desk flying in all directions. "You can go, you can go! Leave it a week before you go back to see Dr. Hurlingford, eh?"

Sydney was warmer and moister than the Blue Mountains, and the day was fine and clear. Emerging onto Macquarie Street with Una at her side, Missy blinked in the brightness.

"Nearly half past eleven," said Una. "Shall we go and sell our share certificates first? The address is in Bridge Street, which is only round the corner from here."

So they did that, and it was remarkably easy. However, the small office and its surly clerk offered no clue as to the identity of the mystery buyer; the most intriguing aspect of the sale was that they were paid in gold sovereigns rather than in paper money. And four hundred gold coins were very heavy, as Missy discovered once she had put them in her bag.

"We can't walk far loaded down like this," said Una, "so I suggest we lunch at the Hotel Metropole – we're only a hop skip and jump away from it – then catch a tram back to

Central and just go tamely home."

In all her life Missy had never eaten in a restaurant, even her Aunt Julia's tea room, nor had she ever been inside the Hurlingford Hotel. So the opulent vastness of the Metropole staggered her, with its crystal chandeliers and marble columns; it also reminded her of Aunt Aurelia's house, because it was beautifully greened and silenced with potted Kentia palms. As for the food – Missy had never tasted anything as delicious as the crayfish salad Una ordered for her.

"I think I might be able to get fat, if I could eat food like this every day," said Missy ecstatically.

Una smiled at her without pity, but with a great deal of understanding. "Poor Missy! Life has passed you by, hasn't it? Now me, life ran over like a through train. Bang boom crash, and there's our Una flat on her face in the water. But cheer up, darling, do! Life won't always pass you by, I promise. You just hang onto the thought that every dog has its day, even the bitches. Only don't let life run you over, either – that's equally hard to deal with."

Wanting to tell Una how very much she liked her, but too inhibited to do so, Missy sought around for an acceptable topic of conversation. "You haven't asked me what the doctor said."

Una's bright blue eyes gleamed. "What did he say?"

Missy sighed. "My heart is as sound as a bell."

"Are you sure?"

Knowing exactly what Una was implying, she smiled. "All right, yes, it is a bit affected. But not by a disease."

"I think it's the worst disease in the world!"

"Not in a doctor's book."

"If you like John Smith so terribly much, why don't you show him you like him?"

"*Me?*"

"Yes, darling, you! You know, your real trouble is that you've been brought up – along with that whole town – to think that if you don't look and act like Alicia Marshall, no man could ever be interested. But my dear, Alicia Marshall does not slay every man who meets her! There are many men with more taste and discrimination than that, and I happen to know that John Smith is one of them." She smiled impishly. "In fact, I think you'd suit John Smith extremely well."

"Is he married?"

"He was at one time, but he's respectably single now – his wife died."

"Oh! Was she – was she nice?"

Una thought about that. "Well, at any rate *I* liked her. There were plenty who didn't."

"Did he like her?"

"I think he probably liked her well enough in the beginning, but not nearly well enough in the end."

"Oh."

Una commandeered the bill and would hear none of

Missy's protests. "Darling, your transactions this morning have been quite without personal reward, where mine have netted me one hundred wonderful pounds that I intend to fritter away like a king's mistress. Lunch is therefore my treat."

A very exclusive-looking dress shop occupied the corner where they waited for the tram, but to Missy's surprise, Una displayed no interest.

"First of all, darling, a hundred pounds wouldn't buy the smell of an oil rag in there," she explained. "Besides which, their clothes are as deplorably dull as their prices are deplorably expensive. No red dresses! It's far too respectable a shop."

"One day I shall have my scarlet lace dress and hat," said Missy, "no matter how unrespectable I look."

"So I don't have heart trouble at all," said Missy to her mother and aunt. "In fact, my heart is perfect." Both the big pale faces turned anxiously to Missy fell instantly into repose.

"Oh, that is good news!" said Octavia.

"What is the matter, then?" asked Drusilla.

"I have a pinched nerve in my spine."

"Good heavens! Does that mean there's no cure?"

"No, Dr. Parkinson thinks he may already have cured me. He almost screwed my head off, there was a horrible sort of crunch, and I should be quite well from now on.

He referred to what he did as a manipulation, I think. But if I do get more attacks, I have to get you to tie two bricks to each of my feet, and I have to hang in the air with my chin resting on a bar!" She grinned. "The mere thought is enough to cure any complaint!" Only with a hefty swing did she manage to deposit her handbag on the table. "Here's something a lot more important – look!" And she withdrew four neatly wrapped cylinders. "One hundred pounds for you, Mother, all in gold. And the same for Aunt Octavia, Aunt Cornelia, and Aunt Julia."

"It's a miracle," said Drusilla.

"No, it's a little tardy justice," contradicted Missy. "You will buy that Singer sewing machine now, won't you?"

Prudence warred with desire in Drusilla's breast until she declared a temporary truce with the outcome undecided. "I said I would think about it, and I will."

When bedtime came around Missy found herself sleepless, despite the day's novel exertions; she lay content-edly in the dark and thought about John Smith. So he had been married, but his wife was dead. There could surely have been no children, or he would surely have them with him for at least part of the time. That was sad, so too was Una's opinion of the union, that he had not liked his wife nearly well enough in the end. Sydney society, decided Missy, was not conducive to happy marriages, what with Una and her Wallace, and John Smith and his dead wife. Still, Mrs. John Smith had not had to suffer the stigma of divorce; at which point, Missy wondered for the first time in her convention-hedged life whether the stigma of divorce might not be preferable to the finality of death.

By midnight her plan was all worked out, and her mind was made up. She would do it, and she would do it tomorrow. After all, what did she have to lose? If her scheme did not bear fruit, she would simply have to continue for the next thirty-three years as she had gone on for the last thirty-three years. Certainly it was worth a try.

Somewhere in her suddenly sleepy brain a little thought was spared for John Smith, the unsuspecting victim. Was it fair? Yes, came the answer. Missy turned over and went to sleep with no further misgivings.

Drusilla elected to bear the four hundred pounds into Byron without assistance, and set off the next morning at nine o'clock, the heavy burden of her bag seeming as a feather. She was very happy, not only for herself, but for her sisters also. In the last few weeks more good fortune had come her way than in the last almost four decades, and she was beginning to dare to hope that the good fortune was a trickle building into a rivulet rather than a splash draining into the sand. But it cannot be for me alone, she vowed. Somehow I must ensure it embraces *all* of us.

While Octavia pottered happily in the kitchen, Missy quietly packed her scant clothing into the battered carpet-bag which served all the ladies of Missalonghi on the rare occasions a bag was needed. On the top cover of her bed she left a note for her mother, then she let herself out of the front door, walked down the path to the gate, and turned left, not right.

This time she didn't timidly explore the start of the descent into John Smith's valley; she walked down it with decision and purpose, using a strong stick and the carpetbag to keep her balance on the treacherous rubble. At the bottom of the landslide the going became easier as the road plunged into the forested flanks below the cliffs. It was not nearly as cold as she imagined it might be, for the ramparts far above took the brunt of the wind; down on the valley floor, all was still and calm.

Four miles from the commencement of the descent the more open woodland of the sloping flanks turned into a kind of jungle, thick with vines and creepers and tree-ferns, even several varieties of palm. There were bellbirds everywhere, though try as she would, she couldn't see them; but their calls filled the air with the most delicate silvery chimes, thin and clear and elfin, utterly unbirdlike. And other birdsongs wove through the chimes, long carols from magpies, joyous trills from tiny fantails which fluttered only inches from her face and seemed to be welcoming her into their home.

That third hour of walking was very damp, the sun hardly showing through the canopy of leaves above, the track slippery from moss and mud and decaying forest detritus. When the first leech dropped on her and immediately attached its skinny slimy wriggling body to her hand, Missy's impulse was to screech and run in demented circles, especially after all her frantic efforts to dislodge it proved vain. But she made herself stand absolutely still and absolutely silent until the hair on her neck and arms subsided, then she gave herself a severe lecture; if these disgusting things lived in John Smith's forest, then she must cope with them in a way that would not brand her in his eyes as a silly woman. The leech had begun to swell up plumply, and, as she discovered when she began to feel areas of exposed skin on neck and face, had been joined by several equally vampirish brothers. Wretched things! They wouldn't let go! So she moved on in the hope that she would encounter fewer leeches moving than standing in one spot, a hope that was right. Replete, the first one to land detached itself without fuss and flopped to the ground, as did its brothers. She then learned that staunch the wounds as she would, they kept on bleeding away. What a sight she must look! Covered in blood. Lesson number one about dreams versus reality.

Shortly afterwards the sound of the river began to fill the distance, and Missy's courage started to bleed away as rapidly as her leech wounds; it took more resolution and strength to walk those last few hundred yards than to mount the whole expedition.

There it was, just around the next bend. A low small cabin built of wattle-and-daub, with a roof of wooden shingles and a lean-to off to one side that looked to be of more recent construction. However, the cabin had a sandstone chimney, and a thin blur of smoke smudged the perfect blue of the sky. He was home, then!

Since it was no part of her plan to pounce on him unaware, Missy stopped at the edge of the clearing and called his name several times in her loudest voice. Two horses grazing in a fenced-off yard lifted their heads to gaze at her curiously before going back to the endless business of feeding, but of John Smith there was no sign. He must be off somewhere, then. She sat down on a convenient tree stump to wait.

The wait wasn't long, for she arrived a little before one o'clock, and he came merrily whistling back to the cabin to get himself some lunch. Even after he entered the clearing he didn't see her; she was sitting in line with the horses, where he struck off towards the river flowing in noisy cascades behind the cabin.

"Mr. Smith!" she called.

He stopped in his tracks, did not move for a moment, then turned. "Oh, bloody hell!" he said.

When he reached her, he scowled at her horribly, not a scrap of welcome in his eyes.

"What are you doing here?"

Missy gulped in a big breath of much-needed air; it was now or never. "Will you marry me, Mr. Smith?" she asked, enunciating very distinctly.

His anger fled at once, replaced by unconcealed mirth.

"It's a long walk down, so you'd better come in and have a cup of tea, Miss Wright," he said, eyes dancing. A finger flicked at the blood on her face. "Leeches, eh? I'm surprised you lasted the distance."

His hand went under her elbow and he walked her at a sedate pace across the clearing without saying another word, just muffling his laughter. The cabin had no verandah, unusual in that part of the world, and, as Missy saw when she entered its dimness, the floor was of packed earth, the fittings spartan. However, for a bachelor establishment it looked remarkably neat and clean, no dirty dishes, no untidiness. A new cast-iron cooking range filled half the chimney, an open fireplace the other half; there was a wooden bench for his washing-up dish, as well as a long rough-hewn table and two straight kitchen chairs. He had made his bed from timber slabs, piled what looked like at least three mattresses on top, and a feather quilt that ought to keep him warm in any weather. Some cow hide stretched across a chunky wooden frame served him as an easy-chair, and his clothing hung on wooden pegs hammered into the wall next to his bed. There were no curtains on the one window, which looked as if it had been recently glazed.

"But why have curtains?" Missy asked aloud.

"Eh?" In the act of lighting two kerosene lamps from a spill he had thrust into the stove, he looked at her.

"How splendid to live in a house that doesn't need any curtains," said Missy.

He put one lamp on the table and the other on an orange crate beside his bed, then busied himself making tea.

"There's really enough light," said Missy, "without lamps."

"You're sitting in front of the window, Miss Wright, and I want some light on your face."

So Missy lapsed into silence, letting her eyes wander wherever they chose, from John Smith to his dwelling and back again. As usual he smelled clean, though dust and earth on his clothing and arms suggested that he had been doing something fairly strenuous all morning, as did a long superficial graze on the back of his left hand and wrist.

He served the tea in enamel mugs and the biscuits still in their huge gaudy tin, but he did everything without apology and with no physical awkwardness. After he had served her and she had indicated she wished for nothing else, he carried his mug and a fistful of biscuits to the leather easy-chair, which he pulled round so he could sit facing her at close quarters.

"Why on earth, Miss Wright, would you want to marry me?"

"Because I love you!" said Missy, her tone astonished.

This answer threw him into confusion; as if suddenly he didn't wish her to see what might lie in his eyes, he removed his gaze from her person to the window behind her, frowning.

"That's ridiculous," he said at last, chewing his lip.

"I would have said it was obvious."

"You can't possibly love someone you don't even know, woman! It's ridiculous."

"I know quite enough about you to love you," she said earnestly. "I know that you're very kind. You're strong on the inside. You're clean. You're different. And you – you have enough *poetry* in you to want to live here of all places."

He blinked. "Christ!" he exclaimed, and laughed. "I must say that's the most interesting catalogue of virtues I've ever been privileged to hear. I like the clean bit best."

"It's important," said Missy gravely.

For a moment he looked as if amusement might get the better of him again, but with an effort he remained sober, and said, "I'm afraid I can't marry you, Miss Wright."

"Why?"

"Why? I'll tell you why," he said, leaning forward in his chair. "You are looking at a man who has found happiness for the first time in his life! If I were twenty, that would be a stupid statement, but I'm pushing fifty, Miss Wright, and that means I'm entitled to some happiness. I'm finally doing all the things I've always wanted to do and never had the time or the chance – and I'm *alone*! No wife, no relations, no dependents of any kind. Not even a dog. Just me. And I love it! To have to share it would spoil it. In fact, I'm going to put a bloody great gate across the top of my road and keep the whole world out. *Marriage?* Not in a fit!"

"It wouldn't be for very long," said Missy quietly.

"A day would be too long, Miss Wright."

"I understand how you feel, Mr. Smith, and I do mean that most sincerely. I too have spent a confined life, I too have chafed against it. But I cannot imagine for a moment that your life has been as dull, as drab and uneventful as mine has always been. Oh, I don't wish to imply that I've been mistreated, or treated one iota worse than the other ladies of Missalonghi. We all live the same dull drab uneventful life. But I am tired of it, Mr. Smith! I want to live a little before I die! Can you understand that?"

"Hell, who couldn't? But if you're in a proposing mood, why not put the hard word on some of the widowers or bachelors in Byron? There must be a few around somewhere." His shell of hardness was setting with every word he said, and he was beginning to feel as if he might extricate himself from this most embarrassing situation without losing either his freedom or his self-respect.

"That would be a fate worse than Missalonghi, because it would be no different. I've chosen you because you're living exactly the kind of life I want to live – away from people, away from houses and smugness and gossip. Believe me, Mr. Smith, I have no intention of cramping your style – on the contrary, I want you to free up mine! I won't be a millstone around your neck. In fact, I'll guarantee to leave you alone most of the time. And it wouldn't be forever, I promise you. A year. Just one little year!"

"So after a year of living the sort of life you're dying to

live, you're going to pick up and tamely go back to the life you hate?" His tone was sceptical.

Missy drew up her meagre form with profound dignity. "I only have a year to live, Mr. Smith," she said.

He looked desperately sorry for her, as if he now knew everything about her there was to know.

She pushed her advantage relentlessly. "I understand very well your reluctance to share this paradise – if it were mine, I too would guard it jealously. But try to see my side, please! I am thirty-three years old, and I have never known any of the things most women my age either take for granted or wish they didn't have at all. I am an old maid! That is the most dreadful fate a woman can suffer, for it goes hand in hand with poverty and lack of beauty. If I had suffered one without the other, some man would have been prepared to marry me, but to suffer both is to be completely undesirable. Yet I *know* that if I can only get past these handicaps, I have a great deal to offer that most women don't, because they have no need to. You would enjoy all the advantages, Mr. Smith, for I would be tied to you by the bonds of gratitude and thankfulness, as well as by love. I wish there was some way right at this moment whereby I could show you how little you'd lose by marrying me, and how much you'd gain you don't even know about. I have good sense, and no puffed-up notion of my own importance. And I would try with might and main to be the nicest of companions for you, as well as the most loving."

He got up abruptly and went to stand looking out the door, his hands clasped behind his back. "Women," he said, "are liars, cheats, connivers and fools. I wouldn't care if I never saw another woman as long as I lived. As for love – I don't *want* to be loved! I just want to be left alone!" This cry from the heart he seemed to think was enough, then, rethinking, he added harshly, "How do I know you're telling me the truth?"

"Well, Mr. Smith, you are not exactly at the top of the list of Byron's most eligible men! I have heard you described as everything from a jailbird to an eccentric, and it is common knowledge that you are not rich. Why therefore should I lie?" She opened her purse and fished out the neatly folded piece of paper she had appropriated from Dr. Parkinson's desk, then got up from her chair and walked across to join him at the door. "Here. Read this. You do know I'm ill, because you were there when I had my first bad turn. And when I met you the other day on my walk, I'm sure I told you I had to go to Sydney to see a heart specialist. Well, this is his report on my condition. I stole it, first of all because I don't want my mother and aunt to know I'm so sick. I don't want to become an object of worry for them, I don't want to be forced into bed and fussed over. So I told them I had a kinked spinal nerve, and if I can keep up the deception, that's what they're going to go on thinking is wrong with me. My second reason for stealing it concerns you. I knew I was going to ask you to marry me and I knew I'd need proof of my sincerity. There is no name on it except the doctor's, I know, but if you look at it carefully, you will see no patient's name has been erased from it, either."

He took the paper, unfolded it, read it quickly and turned to face her. "Aside from being awfully skinny, you look healthy enough to me," he said doubtfully.

Missy did some fast thinking, and prayed he was no medical expert. "Why, between my turns I am healthy enough! Mine is not the sort of heart trouble that saps the strength, it's more like – like – like having little strokes. The valves – stick – and – and when they do, the blood stops flowing. That I gather is what's going to kill me. I don't know any more than that – doctors never want to tell you anything. I suppose they find it hard enough to tell you you're going to die." She heaved a sigh, and began to scale histrionic heights with the aplomb of an actress. "I shall just go out like a light one day!" Her eyes lifted to his wistfully. "I don't want to die at Missalonghi!" she cried pitifully. "I want to die in the arms of the man I love!"

He was a born fighter, so he tried a different tack. "How about a second opinion? Doctors can be wrong."

"What for?" countered Missy. "If I only have a year to live, I do not want to spend it traipsing from one doctor to another!" A big tear fell down her cheek, while others still swimming with telling effect threatened to follow its lead. "Oh, Mr. Smith, I want to spend my last year *happily*!"

He groaned the groan of a condemned man. "For God's sake, woman, don't cry!"

"Why not?" sobbed Missy, scrabbling up her sleeve for her handkerchief. "I think I have every right to cry!"

"Then cry, damn you!" he said, goaded beyond endurance, and marched out of the door.

Missy stood mopping her tears, eyes following him through them as he strode to the far side of the clearing and then disappeared from view. Head down, she returned to her chair and finished her cry with no more appreciative audience than a large blow-fly. After which, she didn't know what to do. Was he coming back? Was he hiding somewhere watching to see her leave before coming back?

Suddenly she felt very tired, utterly dispirited. All that, and no result. So much for Una's encouragement. So much for stolen reports. So much for her bright vision of emancipation. She sighed, and had never meant a sigh more, or sighed more. No use staying here. She wasn't wanted.

She let herself out of the cabin quietly, and made sure that she closed the door. It was gone two o'clock, and she had a nine-mile walk, all uphill, all difficult terrain; it would be late before she arrived back at Missalonghi.

"Yet I don't feel sorry I tried," she said aloud. "It was worth a try, I *know* it was."

"Miss Wright!"

She turned, hope kindling and blazing.

"Hold on, I'll drive you home."

"Thank you, I can walk," she said, not stiffly or huffily, just in her old colourlessly polite manner.

By this he had reached her side, and put his hand beneath her elbow. "No, it's too late and too hard a walk, especially for you. Sit here while I harness up." And he deposited her on the same tree stump where she had sat waiting for him.

She really was too tired to argue, and perhaps too tired to face the walk, so she made no demur. When he was ready, he lifted her up into the cart as easily as if she had been a child.

"This only goes to prove what I've been telling myself lately," he said as he turned the horses out of the clearing onto the track. "I need a smaller vehicle, a sulky or a gig. It's a damned nuisance to have to use both horses and a big cart unless I've got a heavy load."

"Yes, I'm sure you're right," she said meaninglessly.

"Angry?"

Her face turned to his, its expression purely surprised. "No! Why should I be?"

"Well, you didn't meet with much luck, did you?"

She laughed, not very heartily, yet still a genuine laugh. "Poor Mr. Smith, you don't understand at all."

"Obviously I don't. What's the joke?"

"I had nothing to lose. Nothing!"

"Did you really think you might win?"

"I was sure I would win."

"Why?"

"Because you're you."

"And what does that mean?"

"Oh — just that you're so very kind. A decent person."

"Thanks."

After that little was said; the horses plodded reluctantly along the jungly track, obviously not understanding why they were proceeding away from home. But even when they came to the switchback up the landslide they plodded on without visible protest, which to the country-wise Missy indicated that they knew their master better than to baulk. Yet he was pleasant to them, and didn't ply the whip; he dominated them by the force of his will.

"I must say that it shows, your not being a Hurlingford," he said abruptly as the journey neared its end.

"*Not* a Hurlingford? What makes you assume that?"

"Lots of things. Your name, for a start. Your appearance. The godforsaken position of your home, and the lack of money in it. Your nice nature." He sounded as if he grudged this last admission.

"Not all Hurlingfords are rich, Mr. Smith. As a matter of fact I am a Hurlingford, at least on the distaff side. My aunt and mother are the sisters of Maxwell and Herbert Hurlingford, and first cousins of Sir William's."

He turned to stare at her while she explained this, then whistled. "Well, that's a smack in the eye! A nest of genuine Hurlingfords all the way out at the end of Gordon Road, and scraping to make ends meet. What happened?"

So for the rest of the way home Missy regaled John Smith with an account of the perfidy of the first Sir William, and the compounded perfidy of his successors.

"Thank you," he said at the end of it. "You've answered a lot of questions for me, and given me quite a bit to think about." He pulled his horses up outside the front gate of Missalonghi. "Here you are, home again, and well before your mother would be worried."

She jumped down without assistance. "Thank you, dear Mr. Smith. It's as I still maintain – you're a very kind man."

In answer, he tipped his hat and flashed her a smile, then began turning his horses.

Octavia found Missy's note when she went to investigate Missy's whereabouts. There it sat, very white against the brown coverlet, with the single word MOTHER printed across its surface. Her heart thudded down into her boots; notes that said MOTHER never contained good news.

So when she heard Drusilla letting herself in through the front door, she scuttled into the hall with the note in her hand and her protuberant pale blue eyes all geared up to shed as many tears as the contents of the note dictated.

"Missy's gone, and she's left this note for you!"

Drusilla frowned, unalarmed. "Gone?"

"*Gone!* She has taken all her clothes, and she has taken our carpetbag."

The skin over Drusilla's cheeks began to prickle and

stretch uncomfortably; she snatched the note from Octavia and read it aloud so Octavia could not misinterpret the contents.

"Dear Mother," it said,

"Please forgive me for going off without a word, but I really think it is better that you do not know what I plan until I know whether or not it's going to work. I will probably be home tomorrow or the next day for a visit at least. Please do not worry. I am safe. Your loving daughter, Missy."

Octavia's tears overflowed, but Drusilla did not weep. She folded the letter again and carried it into the kitchen, where she propped it very carefully on the shelf of the chimney.

"We must call in the police," said Octavia tearfully.

"We will do no such thing," contradicted Drusilla, and moved the kettle to the front of the stove. "Oh, dear, I need a cup of tea badly!"

"But Missy might be in danger!"

"I very much doubt it. There's nothing in her note to indicate any kind of foolishness." She sat down with a sigh. "Octavia, *do* dry your eyes! The events of the last few days have taught me that Missy is a person to be reckoned with. I have no doubt that she is safe, and that, probably tomorrow, we will indeed see her again. In the meantime, we do not so much as mention to anybody that Missy has left home."

"But she's out there somewhere without a soul to protect her from Men!"

"It may well be that Missy has decided she would rather

not be protected from Men," said Drusilla dryly. "Now do as you're told, Octavia, stop crying and make us some tea. I have a lot to tell you that has nothing to do with Missy's disappearance."

Curiosity overcame distress; Octavia poured a little hot water into the teapot and set it to stand by the stove. "Oh, what?" she asked eagerly.

"Well, I gave Cornelia and Julia their money, and I bought myself a Singer sewing machine."

"Drusilla!"

And so the two ladies left at Missalonghi drank their tea and discussed the events of the day more thoroughly, after which they went back to their routines, and eventually retired to their respective bedrooms.

"Dear God," said Drusilla on her knees, "please help and protect Missy, keep her from all harm and give her strength in all adversities. Amen."

After which she climbed into her bed, the only double one, as befitted the only married lady. But it was some time before she managed to close her eyes.

The organ had saved Missy from detection when John Smith dropped her back at Missalonghi; no one heard his cart arrive or depart, and no one heard Missy as she crept around the side of the house and headed across the backyard towards the shed. It held no place capable of concealing her, but she managed to tuck the carpetbag down behind a sack of fodder, and then she left the shed for the shelter of the orchard until after her mother had milked the cow. Of course the cow knew her step and began to low pitifully to be milked, but before Buttercup became really agitated, out came Drusilla with the bucket.

Missy huddled down behind the fattest-trunked apple tree and closed her eyes and wished she did have terminal heart disease, preferably severe enough to ensure she would never see the morning.

Not until after full darkness had fallen did she stir; it was the penetrating Blue Mountains cold spring air drove her from the orchard at last, into the relative warmth of the shed. Buttercup was lying with feet tucked under, placidly chewing cud, udder comfortably empty. So Missy put a clean sack down on the ground next to the cow, and curled up on the sack with her head and shoulders lying against Buttercup's warm rumbly side.

Of course she should have gathered up her courage and walked into the house the minute John Smith had gone, but when she tried to make her feet mount the front verandah steps, they just would not. How could you tell your mother that you'd proposed marriage to a near-stranger and been refused for your pains? Or failing that one, what convincing story could she have concocted? Missy was not a story spinner, she was only a story reader. Maybe in the morning she could confess, she told herself, gasping at the ache and sorrow of it; but how much worse would that be, with a night spent elsewhere than under the roof of Missalonghi to be accounted for? Who would ever believe she had spent it sleeping with a *cow*? Go inside at once, whispered her better self; but her worse self could not find the courage.

The tears began to gather and to fall, for indeed Missy was exhausted, not so much from her physical exertions as from the terrific burst of will that had sent her to see John Smith.

"Oh, Buttercup, what am I going to do?" she wept.

Buttercup merely huffed.

And shortly afterwards, Missy fell asleep.

The Missalonghi rooster woke her about an hour before dawn, screeching his clarion from the beam right above her head. She leaped up, confused, then subsided against her living pillow in a fresh agony of pain and bewilderment. She wasn't hungry, she wasn't thirsty. What to do? Oh, what to do?

But by dawn she had made up her mind what to do, and rose then to her feet with purpose in her movements. Pulling comb and brush from the carpetbag, she tidied herself as best she could, but at the end of her efforts was dismally aware she smelled strongly of cow.

No sound of stirring life came from Missalonghi as she crept past it, and faintly from out her mother's window came a series of little snores. Safe.

Down once more into John Smith's valley, not with the dreamy enchantment of yesterday, nor with the irrepressible happiness of yesterday, when nothing had seemed impossible and everything had seemed bound to end well. This time Missy marched with little hope but iron determination; he would not say her nay again, even if it meant she had to spend every night of the next year in her mother's shed with Buttercup for a bedmate, and every day marching down to the bottom of John Smith's valley to ask again. For ask again she would, and tomorrow if he said nay today, and the day after, and the day after that...

It was going on for ten o'clock when she came at last to the clearing and the cabin; there rose the same rippling blur from the chimney, but, as yesterday, no John Smith. Down on the tree stump she sat to wait.

Perhaps he too had passed beyond hunger; when noon came and went without a sign of him, Missy resigned herself to waiting the whole afternoon as well. Indeed, the sun had long gone behind the great walls above, and the light was fading rapidly, before he came home. More seriously than yesterday, but just as blind to Missy sitting on her stump.

"Mr. Smith!"

"Bloody hell!"

He came across immediately to stand looking down at her, not angrily, but not pleasantly, either. "What are you doing back here again?"

"Will you marry me, Mr. Smith?"

This time he didn't put his hand beneath her elbow and walk her across to the cabin; he turned to face her fully as she rose to her feet, and looked down into her eyes.

"Is someone putting you up to this?" he asked.

"No."

"Does it really mean that much to you?"

"It means my life, literally. I am not going home! I'm going to come here every day and ask again."

"You're playing with fire, Miss Wright," he said, lips thin and tight. "Hasn't it occurred to you that a man might resort to violence if a woman refuses to leave him alone?"

She smiled up serenely, sublimely, seraphically. "Some men, maybe. But not you, Mr. Smith."

"What do you really stand to gain? What if I did say I'd marry you? Is that the sort of husband you want, a man you've worn down until he doesn't know what else to do for peace than give in – or strangle you?" His voice dropped, became very hard. "In this big wide world, Miss Wright, lives a malignant thing called *hate*. I beg of you, don't uncage it!"

"Will you marry me?" she asked.

He screwed up his mouth, blew air through his nose, and lifted his head to stare above hers at something she couldn't see. And said nothing for what seemed like a very long time. Then he shrugged, looked down at her. "I admit I've thought a lot about you since yesterday, and even the heaviest work I could find didn't stop my thinking about you. And I started to wonder too if maybe I was being offered a way to atone, and if my luck might disappear because I ignored the offer."

"A way to atone? Atone for what?"

"Just a figure of speech. Everyone has something to

atone for, no one is free of guilt. In forcing yourself on me, you're creating a cause for atonement, don't you see that?"

"Yes."

"But it makes no difference?"

"I'll take whatever comes to me gladly, Mr. Smith, if I can take you along with it."

"Very well, then. I'll marry you."

All of Missy's pain and numbness flew away. "Oh, thank you, Mr. Smith! You won't regret it, I promise!"

He grunted. "You're a child, Miss Wright, not a grown woman, and perhaps that's why I've given in rather than strangled you. I can't honestly believe there's woman's guile in you. Only don't ever give me reason to change that opinion."

And now his hand went under her arm, the signal to walk.

"There's one thing I must ask, Mr. Smith," she said.

"What?"

"That we never refer to the fact that I'm going to die, nor let it influence our behaviour. I want to be free! And I cannot be free if I am to be perpetually reminded by word or deed that I'm going to die."

"Agreed," said John Smith.

Not wanting to push her luck, for she sensed she had gone about as far in that line as was prudent, Missy entered the cabin and went to sit quietly in one of the kitchen chairs, while John Smith swung round inside the door and stood staring out of it at the beginnings of a thin blue night's ground mist.

Silently she watched his back, which was long and broad and, at the moment, extremely eloquent. But after about five minutes she ventured to say, her voice very small and apologetic, "What happens now, Mr. Smith?"

He jumped as if he had forgotten she was there, and went to sit opposite her at the table. His face in the gloom was full of shadows, heavy, deadened, a little daunting. But when he spoke, it was cheerfully enough, as if he had decided there was no point in making himself more miserable than the situation called for. "My name is John," he said, and got up to light his two lamps, both of which he placed on the table so he could see her face. "As to the main business, we get a licence, and we get married."

"How long will it take?"

He shrugged. "I don't know, if banns aren't called. A couple of days? Maybe even sooner, with a special licence. In the meantime, I'd better drive you home."

"Oh, no! I'm staying here," said Missy.

"If you stay here you're likely to start your honeymoon prematurely," he said, hope blossoming. What a good idea! She might decide she didn't like it! After all, most women didn't. And he could be hard about it, not rape her exactly, just force her a little; a virgin of her age was bound to be easy to frighten. At which point he made the mistake of looking at her to see how she reacted. And there she was, poor little dying thing, just gazing at him with blinded foolish affection, like a puppy awash with love. John Smith's sleeping heart moved, felt a bitter and unaccustomed pain. For indeed she had haunted him all day, no matter how hard he worked to drive out her image and replace it by emptiness hacked out of physical labour. He had his secrets, some of them buried so deep he could tell himself in all truth that he had never suffered those secrets, that he was reborn in all the newness and nakedness of a life begun again. But all day things had nibbled and whispered and gnawed, and the utter pleasure he had found in his valley had vanished. Maybe he did have to atone; maybe that was why she had come. Only he honestly didn't have one thing to atone for so large, so depressing. He didn't. Oh no, he didn't, he didn't!

Maybe she wouldn't like it. Take her to bed, John Smith, show her what it's like in the wasteland of the body, fill her with yourself and with disgust for it. She's a woman.

But Missy liked it very well, and demonstrated a surprising aptitude for it. Another nail went thudding into John Smith's coffin, as he wryly admitted to himself about three hours after he and Missy had retired dinnerless to bed. Wonders never ceased. This ageing spinster virgin was made for it! Though dreadfully ignorant at first, she was neither shy nor shamed, and her affectionate responses warmed him, touched him, made it impossible for him to be cruel or unkind to her. The little baggage! None of your lying there passively with your legs open for her! And how much

154

life there was in her, just waiting to be tapped. Suddenly the thought that the end of her life was imminent shocked him; it was one thing to pity someone he didn't know, quite another to face the same dilemma with someone he knew intimately. That was the trouble with beds. They turned strangers into intimates more quickly than ten years of polite teas in parlours.

Missy slept like a log and woke before John Smith did, probably because sleep eluded him long after it had claimed her. He had more to think about.

A faint light filtered through the window, so she eased herself carefully out of the bed and stood shivering until she donned the dressing gown out of her bag. How lovely it had been! More of a realist than she had suspected, she dismissed the initial unpleasantness of pain and remembered instead those big strong work-roughened hands stroking and soothing and comforting. Feelings and sensations, touches and kisses, heat and light – oh yes, it was lovely!

She moved as quietly as she could about the cabin, hotting up the stove and moving the kettle to a place where it would boil. But of course her activity woke him, and he got out of bed too, quite unconcerned at his nakedness; Missy was given an unparalleled opportunity to study the anatomical differences between men and women.

Even more delightful than this was his reaction to her presence. He walked straight across to her, folded her in his arms and stood rocking gently, still half-asleep and thus

COLLEEN McCULLOUGH

heavy against her, his beard scraping her neck.

"Good morning," she whispered, her smiling lips pressing little kisses on his shoulder.

"Morning," he mumbled, evidently liking her response.

Of course she was ravenous, having had virtually nothing to eat in two days. "I'll get breakfast," she said.

"Want a bath?" He sounded more awake, but made no attempt to move away from her.

He could smell Buttercup! Oh, poor man! Hunger fled yet again. "Yes, please. But a lavatory too?"

"Get your shoes on."

While she slid her feet into her boots, not bothering to lace them, he rummaged in a big chest and produced two towels, old and rough, but clean.

The clearing sparkled with frost and was still in heavy shade, but as Missy looked up, the great sandstone walls of the valley were already glowing red with the sunrise, and the sky was taking on the muted milky radiance of a pearl – or of Una's skin. Birds called and sang everywhere, never more prone to give voice than at dawn.

"The lavatory's a bit primitive," he warned, showing her where he had dug a deep hole and placed some stone blocks around it for a seat, with newspaper tucked into a box to keep it dry; he had not enclosed it with roof or walls.

"It's the best-ventilated lavatory I've ever seen," she said cheerfully.

He chuckled. "Long job, or short?"

156

"Short, thank you."

"Then I'll wait for you. Over there." He pointed to the far side of the clearing.

When Missy joined him a minute later she was already shivering in anticipation of an icy plunge into the river; he looked like the kind of man who would relish freezing ablutions. Maybe, she thought, I'll be hoist with my own petard, and keel over stone dead from the shock.

But instead of steering her towards the river, John Smith drew her into the middle of a thicket of tree-ferns and wild clematis in feathery white flower. And there before her was the most beautiful bathroom in the entire world, a warm spring that trickled out of a cleft between two rocks at the top of a small stony incline, and fell, too thinly to be called a cascade, into a wide and mossy basin.

Missy had her robe off in a flash, and two seconds later was stepping down into a crystal-clear pool of blood-heat water, tendrils of steam rising languorously off it into the chilly air. It was about eighteen inches deep, and its bottom was clean smooth rock. No leeches, either!

"Go easy on the soap," advised John Smith, pointing to where a fat cake of his expensive brand sat in a small niche alongside the pool. "The water obviously gets away, because the level of the pool never rises any more than the spring stops flowing, but don't tempt fate."

"Now I understand why you're so clean," she said, thinking of Missalonghi baths, two inches of water in the bottom of the rusting tub, hot from a kettle and cold from a bucket. And that one miserably inadequate ration of water was used by all three ladies, with Missy, the shortest straw, last in line.

Quite unaware how alluring she looked, she smiled up at him and lifted out her arms until the small buff nipples of her slight breasts just rode clear of the water. "Aren't you coming in too?" she asked in the tones of a professional temptress. "There's plenty of room."

He needed no further encouragement, and appeared to forget his strictures about the production of suds, so assiduous was he in making sure every part of her was thoroughly explored with his hand and the bar of soap; nor did she think that his thoroughness had much to do with Buttercup. She submitted with purring pleasure, but then insisted upon returning the service. And so bath-time occupied the best part of an hour.

However, over breakfast he got down to business. "There must be a registry office in Katoomba, so we'll go on in and get a marriage licence," he said.

"If I go only as far as Missalonghi with you and then walk on into Byron and catch the train, I imagine I'll get to Katoomba almost as quickly as you will in your cart," said Missy. "I must see Mother, I want to shop for food, and I have to take a book back to the library."

He looked suddenly alarmed. "You're not by any chance planning a big wedding, are you?"

She laughed. "No! Just you and me will do very well. I left a note for Mother, though, so I want to make sure she's not too upset. And my dearest friend works in the library – would you mind if she came to our wedding?"

"Not if you want her there. Though I warn you, if I can persuade the powers that be, I'd like to get it over and done with today."

"In Katoomba?"

"Yes."

Married in *brown*! Wouldn't it? Missy sighed. "All right, if you'll promise me something."

"What?" he asked warily.

"When I die, will you bury me in a scarlet lace dress? Or if you can't find that, any colour but brown!"

He looked surprised. "Don't you like brown? I've never seen you wear anything else."

"I wear brown because I'm poor but respectable. Brown doesn't show the dirt, it never goes in or out of fashion, it never fades, and it's never cheap or common or trollopy."

That made him laugh, but then he went back to business. "Do you have a birth certificate?"

"Yes, in my bag."

"What's your real name?"

Her reaction was extraordinary; she went red, shifted around on her chair, clenched her teeth. "Can't you just use Missy? It's what I've always been called, honestly."

"Sooner or later your real name is going to have to come

159

out." He grinned. "Come on, make a clean breast of it! It can't be that bad, surely."

"Missalonghi."

He burst out laughing. "You're pulling my leg!"

"I wish I were."

"The same as your house?"

"Exactly the same. My father thought it was the most beautiful word in the world, and he loathed the Hurlingford habit of using Latin names. Mother wanted to call me Camilla, but he insisted on Missalonghi."

"You poor little bitch!"

This time Missy's feet experienced no trouble mounting the steps to the front verandah of Missalonghi; she banged on the door as if she was a stranger.

Drusilla answered, and looked at her daughter as if she really was a stranger. Definitely there was nothing the matter with her! In fact, she looked better than in all her life.

"I know what you've been doing, my girl," she said as she led the way down the hall to the kitchen. "I wish you'd stuck to reading about it, but I daresay that's crying over spilt milk now, eh? Are you back for good?"

"No."

Octavia came hobbling, and received a kiss on either cheek from the sparkling Missy.

"Are you all right?" she quavered, clutching at Missy's hands convulsively.

"Of course she's all right!" said Drusilla bracingly. "*Look* at her, for heaven's sake!"

Missy smiled at her mother lovingly; how odd, that only now the cord binding her to Missalonghi was broken did she understand the depth of her love for Drusilla. But maybe now she had opportunity to stand back and see Drusilla's worries, heartaches, difficulties.

"I thank you very much, Mother," she said, "for according me the dignity of assuming I know what I'm doing."

"At going on thirty-four, Missy, if you don't know what you're doing, there's no hope for you. You tried it our way for long enough, and who's to say your way won't be better?"

"Very true. But what you're telling me now is a far cry from dictating the kind of books I might read, and the colour of my clothes."

"You put up with it tamely enough."

"Yes, I suppose I did."

"You get the government you deserve, Missy, always."

"If you can admit that, Mother, don't you think it's more than time you and the aunts and all the other manless Hurlingford women banded together to do something about the glaring injustices and inequalities in this family?"

"Ever since you told us how Billy has lied to us, Missy, I have been thinking along those lines, I assure you. And I have been talking to Julia and Cornelia too. But there is no law that compels a man – or a woman – to leave property equally divided between sons and daughters. In my book, the worst offenders of all have been Hurlingford women with money to leave – nothing goes to their daughters, not even a house on five acres! So I have always felt there was no chance for us, when our own female kind stand so solidly behind Hurlingford men. It is sad, but it is true."

"You're speaking of the Hurlingford women who will lose a great deal if you win. I'm speaking of our fellow sufferers, and I know you can get them moving if you really try. You do have legal grounds to seek compensation for those unpaid dividends, and I think you should institute proceedings against Uncle Herbert to compel him to disclose the full details of his various investment schemes." Missy shot a demure look at Drusilla from under her lashes. "After all, Mother, you were the one who said it – you get the government you deserve."

She walked from Missalonghi into Byron. What a beautiful, beautiful day! For the first time in her life she felt really well, the bursting out of one's skin sensation she had read about but never experienced; and for the first time in her life she was looking forward to living a long life. That is, until she remembered that the full measure of her happiness depended upon one John Smith, and John Smith only expected to put up with her for a year at most. She had lied and cheated and stolen to feel this happy, and she wasn't at all sorry for it. The Alicias of this world might snap their fingers and conjure up the men of their choice, but no use pretending a man like John Smith would have looked sideways at a Missy Wright, snap though she would. And yet she *knew* she could make John Smith the happiest man – if not in the world – at least in the town of Byron. She had better! Because when her year was up, he had to want her to live so badly he was prepared to forgive her the stealing and the cheating and the lying.

Time was getting on, and she had to make sure she caught the eleven o'clock train into Katoomba, where John Smith had promised to be waiting for her at the station. Groceries she could put off until tomorrow, but somehow she had a feeling Una could not be postponed. To the library it was, then.

A magnificent motorcar was purring sedately down the middle of Byron Street as Missy hurried along in her brown linen dress, inconspicuous as ever. Which was more than could be said for the motorcar, also brown; it had collected an admiring audience down both sides of the road, locals and visitors alike. Glancing at it in amusement, Missy decided the chauffeur had a definite edge over the two occupants of the tonneau when it came to haughty aloofness. The chauffeur she knew from hearsay; a handsome fellow with more love for cutting a fine figure than hard work, and a reputation for treating his many women badly. The occupants of the tonneau she knew from bitter experience; Alicia and Uncle Billy.

Alicia's eyes met hers. The next moment the sumptuous car had slewed sideways into the kerb, and Alicia and

Uncle Billy were tumbling out well ahead of the startled chauffeur's attempt to open a door for them.

"What do you mean, Missy Wright, taking Aunt Cornelia's shares and selling them out from under our noses?" demanded Alicia without preamble, two bright red spots burning in her alabaster cheeks.

"Why shouldn't I?" asked Missy coolly.

"Because it's none of your damned interfering business!" barked Sir William, stiff with outrage.

"It's as much my business as it is yours, Uncle Billy. I knew where I could get Aunt Cornelia ten pounds a share, and what use were they to her when you'd led her to believe they were quite worthless? Aunt Cornelia badly needs an operation on her feet she couldn't afford because, Alicia, I gather you refused to give her either time off or a little extra money. So I sold her shares for a hundred pounds, and now she can have her operation. If you wish to terminate her employment, at least she has a sum in the bank to tide her over until she can find another position – I'm sure there are shops in Katoomba just dying to engage someone of her calibre. You might like to know that I have also sold Aunt Julia's shares, and Aunt Octavia's, and Mother's."

"*What?*" squawked Sir William.

"All of them? You sold all of them?" faltered Alicia, the red spots in her cheeks draining away in a second.

"I most certainly did." Missy stared at her cousin with a malice she had not known she possessed. "Why, Alicia, don't tell me forty little shares in the great big Byron Bottle Company were enough to tip the balance!"

For a confused moment Alicia fancied Missy had grown horns and a tail. "What's the matter with you?" she cried. "You've got to be off your head! Soiling my dress, saying insulting things about me in front of my family, and now selling that family into ruin! You ought to be locked up!"

"I only wish what I did had resulted in your being locked up. Now if you'll both excuse me, I must dash. I have an appointment to be married." And Missy walked away with her nose in the air.

"I think I'm going to faint," announced Alicia, and suited action to words by flopping against Uncle Herbert's window, the one full of work clothes.

Sir William seized the opportunity to put his arms around her, head turned to call for assistance from his chauffeur; but somehow as they supported Alicia between them back to the car, it was the chauffeur's ungloved fingers that managed to ascertain the delicious size and shape of Alicia's nipples. By this time the crowd had swelled to include all of Uncle Herbert's sons and grandsons, so Sir William dumped Alicia unceremoniously on the seat and ordered the chauffeur to drive off immediately.

When her prospective father-in-law attempted to loosen her stays by lifting up her dress and groping inside her fine lawn drawers, Alicia revived in a hurry.

"Stop that, you lecherous old man!" she snapped,

forgetting the need to be tactful, and leaned forward to press her cheeks between her palms. "Oh, lord, I feel awful!"

"Would you like to go home now we don't have to drive out to Missalonghi?" asked Sir William, red-faced.

"Yes, I would." She lay back against the seat and let the cool air fan her skin, and finally relaxed a little, and sighed. Thank heavens! She was beginning to feel better.

Right in front of her but on the other side of the glass that separated the tonneau from the open driving compartment, the chauffeur's proudly shaped head sat upon his strong smooth neck; what lovely ears he had for a man, small and set right against his skull. He was handsome, as dark as Missy, and as alien. It took a brawny man to heft her around as easily as he had, and his hands on her breasts – she felt her nipples pop up at the memory of them, and squirmed achingly on the seat. What was his name? Frank? Yes, Frank. Frank Pellagrino. He used to work at the bottling plant until he got the post as Uncle Billy's chauffeur.

A sidelong glance at Sir William revealed him sitting bolt upright, a very worried man.

"Do those forty shares make so much difference to us?"

"All the difference in the world, now we know Richard Hurlingford sold out a month ago." Sir William sighed. "And it explains why the mystery buyer thinks he has sufficient clout to call an extraordinary meeting tomorrow."

"The little fool!" snarled Alicia. "How could Missy be such a little fool?"

"I think we're the fools, Alicia. I for one never even noticed Missy Wright, but I see now that I should have. And been more attentive to all the ladies of Missalonghi. Did you take in how she looked this morning? As if she'd got to the cream ahead of every other cat in the district. And did she say she had an appointment to be married, or was that my imagination?"

Alicia snorted. "Oh, she said it, but I suspect it was *her* imagination." A more urgent grievance came to mind. "Silly old Auntie Cornie!" she muttered savagely. "Oh, how I wish I could have had the satisfaction this morning of sacking her when she came prattling about her shares and the time she was going to take off for her operation!"

"Well, why didn't you sack her?"

"Because I can't, that's why! My hat shop may well end up my only source of income, if things at the plant keep going from bad to worse. And I'll never find anyone else half so good to run the salon end of it, even if I paid them ten times what I pay Auntie Cornie. She's – indispensable."

"You'd better pray she never realises it, or she'll ask for ten times what you currently pay her." A tinge of satisfaction coloured his voice as he added, "And then, my dear, if you can't afford it, you'll have to go into the shop as your own sales dame. You'd be even better at it than Cornie."

"I can't do that!" gasped Alicia. "It would *ruin* my social standing! It's one thing to be the creative genius behind a business of that nature, but quite another to have to peddle

167

my wares in person." She tugged at the lapels of her pale pink coat, her lovely face set into the lines of sullen discontent its construction made fatally easy. "Oh, Uncle Billy, suddenly I feel as if I'm walking on ice, and it's going to crack any minute, and I'm going to go under!"

"We're in a pickle, it's true. But don't give up, we're not finished yet. Pounds to peanuts, when the mystery buyer turns up to his extraordinary meeting tomorrow, he'll turn out to be some self-made yokel easily manipulated by his betters. And for that sort of exercise, you will come in very handy."

Alicia did not reply, merely flicked him a glance of mingled doubt and dislike; her eyes reverted to the back of the chauffeur's head, a far nicer prospect than Sir William's choleric countenance.

When Missy walked into the library she fully expected to find Una, even though it was not one of Una's days. And sure enough, there was Una.

"Oh, Missy, I'm so glad to see you!" she cried, jumping up. "I have a surprise for you."

"I have a few surprises for you too," said Missy.

"Wait right there, I'll be back in two flicks of a dead lamb's tail." Una vanished into the tea cubicle, and came out bearing a large white box and hatbox, each tied up with white ribbon. "Happy anything, dearest Missy."

They smiled at each other in complete understanding and great affection.

"It's a scarlet lace dress and hat," said Missy.

"It's a scarlet lace dress and hat," agreed Una.

"I shall wear it to my wedding."

"John Smith! You've picked exactly the right man."

"I had to resort to trickery and deception to get him."

"If you couldn't get him any other way, why not?"

"I told him I was dying of heart trouble."

"Aren't we all?"

"That," said Missy, "is splitting hairs. Can you come to my wedding?"

"I'd love to, but no."

"Why?"

"It wouldn't be appropriate."

"Because of your divorce? But we're not getting married in a church, so who can object?"

"It has nothing to do with divorce, darling. I don't think John Smith would appreciate a face from the past at his wedding."

That made sense, therefore Missy left it alone. And there was nothing really left to say; her gratitude was quite beyond words, her need to go quickly was great. Una stood watching her painfully, as if with her she was taking something so precious the quality of Una's life would suffer ever afterwards – and that something was not so tangible as a scarlet lace dress and hat. On an impulse she didn't understand, Missy returned to the desk, leaned over it and put her arm about Una's shoulders, her lips against Una's cheek. So frail, so cold, so weightless!

"Goodbye, Una."

"Goodbye, my best and dearest friend. Be happy!"

Missy made the train with a minute to spare, and saw John
Smith on the platform in Katoomba before the train came
to a standstill. Thank God for that. He hadn't changed his
mind during his slow amble along the highway, then. And
in fact when he saw her alight from her carriage, he even
looked quite glad to see her!

"They'll issue us with a licence and marry us today," he
said, taking Missy's boxes from her.

"And I don't have to be married in brown," said Missy,
retrieving her boxes. "If you'll excuse me, I'll pop into the
platform toilet and change into my wedding dress."

"*Wedding* dress?" He looked down at his grey flannel
work shirt and his old moleskin trousers in comical dismay.

She laughed. "Don't worry, it's not traditional. In fact,
I guarantee that you're going to look a great deal more
appropriate than I am."

Her dress fitted perfectly. What an eye for size Una had!
And what a wonderful colour! Her eyes swam with the
strain of looking at it. Where on earth had Una managed to
find a garment so elegant in style yet so wanton in colour?

The mirror on the wall seemed to own a touch of magic,
for whoever it reflected, it lent a slight patina of beauty;
adjusting her preposterous scarlet hat, Missy decided she

looked very well. Her darkness was suddenly interesting, her thin body was suddenly merely slender as a young tree. Yes, very well! And certainly not spinsterish.

Once he recovered from the shock of that red, John Smith thought she looked very well too. "Now this is my sort of wedding! I look like a hayseed, and you look like a madam." He tucked her arm through his gleefully. "Come on, woman, let's get the deed over before I change my mind."

They strolled into Katoomba Street, the cynosure of all eyes, and actually quite pleased with the sensation they were creating.

"That was easy," said Missy after the deed was done and they were sitting together in John Smith's cart. She held out her hand to see her ring. "I am now Mrs. John Smith. How nice it sounds!"

"I must say this time was a lot better than the last."

"Was your first wedding a big affair, then?"

"It could have passed for a circus. Two hundred and fifty guests, the bride with a thirty-foot train that needed a whole regiment of runny-nosed little boys to lift it, twelve or fourteen bridesmaids, all of the men stuffed into tails, the archbishop of something presiding, a massed choir – God Jesus, at the time it was a nightmare! But compared to what followed, it was an idyll in paradise." He looked sideways at her, one eyebrow raised. "Do you want to hear this?"

"I think I'd better. They say the second wife always has to contend with the ghost of the first, and that it's a lot harder to fight a ghost than a living person." She paused to gather her courage. "Was she – dear to you?"

"She may have been when I married her, I honestly can't remember. I didn't know her, you see. I only knew of her. She must have meant to have me, because I'm sure I didn't do the proposing. I'm obviously the sort of bloke women propose to! Only I didn't mind your way of proposing, at least it was honest and above-board. But her – one minute she was all over me like a rash, the next minute she was acting as if I had the plague. Blowing hot and cold, they call it. I think women think it's expected of them, that if they don't do it, they're going to make life too easy for the bloke. Now that's where I like you very much, Mrs. Smith. You don't blow hot and cold at all."

"I'm too grateful," said Missy humbly. "Do go on! What happened after that?"

He shrugged. "Oh, she decided she was entitled to make all the decisions, that what *she* wanted was all that mattered. Once she'd landed her fish, the fish didn't matter a bit. I was just there to prove she could catch a fish, to lend her respectability, to give her an escort here and there. She didn't exactly have lovers, she had what she called cicisbeos, pansified twerps with gardenias in their buttonholes and a better shine on their hair than on their patent leather shoes. If anyone was ever branded by the company she kept, my first wife certainly was – her women friends were as hard as nails and as tough as old boots, and her men friends were as soft as butter and as limp as last week's lettuce. She liked to mock me. In front of anyone, everyone. I was dull, I was stodgy. And she never kept our differences private, she'd get set on a quarrel no matter how public the place. In a nutshell, she held me in utter contempt."

"And you? What light did you hold her in?"

"I *loathed* her." Evidently he still did, for the feeling in his voice did not belong to an experience buried in the past.

"How long were you married?"

"About four or five years."

"Were there any children?"

"Hell, no! She might have lost her figure. And of course that meant she was a great one for teasing, for kissing and cuddling, but to get my leg over her – it only happened when she got drunk, and afterwards she'd scream and howl and carry on in case anything came of it, then she'd pop out and visit the tame doctor they all patronised."

"And she *died*?" asked Missy, scarcely able to credit that such a woman could have had so much consideration.

"We had a terrible fight one evening over – oh, I don't know, something small and idiotic that actually didn't matter a bit. We lived in a house that had a waterfrontage onto the Harbour, and apparently after I'd gone out she decided to go for a swim to cool her temper. They found her body a couple of weeks later, washed up on Balmoral Beach."

"Oh, poor thing!"

He snorted. "Poor thing, nothing! The police tried in every way they knew to pin it on me, but luckily the minute she'd done shouting at me, I went out, and I met a friend not twenty yards down the road. He'd been kicked out of bed too, so we walked to where he'd been going, the flat of a mutual friend – a bachelor, the wily bastard. There we stayed until past noon of the following day, getting drunker and drunker. And since the servants had seen her alive and well more than half an hour after my friend and I arrived at our mutual friend's flat, the police couldn't touch me. Anyway, after the body turned up the post mortem revealed that she'd died of simple drowning, with no evidence of foul play. Not that that stopped a lot of people in Sydney reckoning I did kill her – I just got a name for being too smart to get caught, and my friends for being bought to alibi me."

"When did all this happen?"

"About twenty years ago."

"A long time! What have you done with yourself since, that it's taken you so long to do what you've always wanted?"

"Well, I quit Australia as soon as the police let go. And I drifted round the world. Africa, the Klondike, China, Brazil, Texas. I had to live through almost twenty years of voluntary exile. Since I was born in London, I changed my name by deed-poll there, and when I did come back to Australia, I came as that bona-fide citizen of the world, John Smith, with all my money in gold and no past."

"Why *Byron*?"

"Because of the valley. I knew it was coming up for sale, and I've always wanted to own a whole valley."

Feeling she had probed enough, Missy changed the subject to the skulduggery going on at the Byron Bottle Company, and told her husband about the plight her mother and aunts were in because of it. John Smith listened most attentively, a smile playing round the corners of his mouth, and when she had ended her tale he put his arm around her, drew her across the seat against his side, and kept her there.

"Well, Mrs. Smith, I really didn't want to marry you when you first brought the subject up, but I confess I'm growing more reconciled to it every time you open your mouth, not to mention your legs," he said. "You're a woman of sense, your heart's in the right place, and you're a Hurlingford of the Hurlingfords, which gives me a lot of power I didn't expect to have," he said. "Interesting, how things turn out."

Missy rode the rest of the way home in blissful silence.

The next morning John Smith donned a suit, a collar, and a tie, all remarkably well cut and oddly smart.

"Whatever it is, it must be a lot more important than your wedding," observed Missy without a trace of resentment.

"It is."

"Are you going far afield?"

"Only to Byron."

"Then if I'm quick about it, may I come as far as Mother's with you, please?"

"Good idea, wife! Wait there for me until some time late this afternoon, and you can introduce me to my in-laws when I pick you up. I'll probably have a lot to say to them."

It's going to be all right, thought Missy as she rode in her bright red dress and hat alongside her unfamiliarly elegant husband up to the top of the ridge. I don't care if I got him by trickery and deceit. He likes me, he really does like me, and without even realising it himself, he's already moved over a little to fit me in alongside him. When my year is up, I'll be able to tell him the truth. Besides, if I'm lucky, I may well by then be the mother of his child. It hurt him badly when his first wife didn't want any, and now he's closer to fifty than to forty, so children will be even more important to him. He will be an excellent father, because he can laugh.

Before they set out for Byron he had taken her across the clearing and round its bend to where he intended to build his house. The waterfall, she discovered, fell so far that on a windy day it never reached the valley floor, spinning away instead into nothingness, and filling the air with clouds of rainbows. Yet there was a huge pool below it, wide and calm until it poured through a narrow defile and became the cascade-tortured river, a pool the colour of a turquoise or of Egyptian faience, opaque as milk, dense as syrup. The source of all this water, he showed her, was a cave below the cliffs, out of which issued a very large underground stream.

"There's an outcropping of limestone here," he explained. "That's why the pool is such a bizarre colour."

"And this is really where we're going to live, looking at so much loveliness?"

"Where *I* will live, anyway. I doubt you'll be here to see it." His face twisted. "Houses don't get built in a day, Missy, especially when they're built single-handed. I don't want a horde of workmen down here, pissing in the pool and getting drunk on Saturdays and then telling any curious bystander what's going on in my valley."

"I thought we had a bargain, not to mention my condition? Anyway, you won't be building single-handed, you'll have my hands as well," said Missy cheerfully. "I'm no stranger to hard work, and the cabin is so small it won't keep me busy. From what the doctor said, it makes no difference whether I lie in a bed or work like a navvy – one day it will happen, that's all."

At which he took her in his arms and kissed her as if he enjoyed kissing her, and as if she was already a little precious to him. They finally set out for Byron somewhat later than originally intended, but neither of them minded.

Octavia and Drusilla were in the kitchen when Missy walked in unannounced. They stared at her in astonishment, trying to take in the full glory of that outlandish scarlet lace dress, not to mention the huge lopsided hat with its graceless plume of scarlet ostrich feathers.

She hadn't turned into a beauty overnight, but there was certainly an eye-catching quality about her, and she held herself too proudly to be mistaken for a trollop. In fact, she looked a lot more like a sophisticated visitor from London than one of the inhabitants of Caroline Lamb Place. There was also no doubting that the colour suited her down to the ground.

"Oh, Missy, you look lovely!" squeaked Octavia, sitting down in a hurry.

Missy kissed her, and kissed her mother. "That's nice to know, Auntie, because I admit I feel lovely." She grinned at them triumphantly. "I came to tell you that I'm married," she announced, waving her left hand under their noses.

"Who?" asked Drusilla, beaming.

"John Smith. We were married yesterday in Katoomba."

Suddenly neither to Drusilla nor Octavia did it matter a scrap that the whole town of Byron called him a jailbird, or worse; he had rescued their Missy from the multiple horrors of spinsterhood, and he must therefore be loved for it with gratitude and respect and loyalty.

Octavia positively leaped up to put the kettle on, moving with more flexibility and ease than she had in years, though Drusilla didn't notice; she was too busy looking at her girl's convincingly massive wedding ring.

"Mrs. John Smith," she said experimentally. "Why, bless my soul, Missy, it sounds quite distinguished!"

"Simplicity usually is distinguished."

"Where is he? When is he coming to see us?" asked Octavia.

"He had some business or other in Byron, but he expects to be done later this afternoon, and he wants to meet you when he picks me up to take me home. I thought, Mother, that to fill in the day, you and I might walk into Byron. I have to buy groceries, and I want to go to Uncle Herbert's to choose some materials for me to make into dresses. Because I am done forever with brown! I won't even wear it to work in. I'm going to work in a man's shirt and man's trousers because they're a great deal more comfortable and sensible, and who's to see me?"

"Isn't it lucky that you bought a Singer sewing machine, Drusilla?" asked Octavia from the stove, too happy at the way things had turned out to worry about the trousers.

But Drusilla had something so important on her mind that neither Singer sewing machines nor trousers could loom larger. "Can you afford it?" she asked anxiously. "I can make for you for nothing, but the materials at Herbert's are so expensive, especially once one gets away from brown!"

"It seems I can indeed afford it. John told me last night that he was going to put a thousand pounds in the bank for me this morning. Because he said a wife shouldn't have to ask her husband for every little penny she needs, nor account for every little penny she spends. All he asked was that I didn't exceed the allowance he makes me – a thousand pounds every year! Can you imagine it? And the housekeeping is separate from that! He put a hundred pounds into an empty Bushell's coffee jar and says he'll keep it replenished, and doesn't want to see the dockets. Oh, Mother, I'm still breathless!"

"A thousand pounds!" Octavia and Drusilla stared at Missy in thunderstruck respect.

"Then he must be a rich man," said Drusilla, and did some rapid mental gymnastics in which she saw herself finally able to cock a snook at Aurelia and Augusta and Antonia. Hah! Not only had Missy beaten Alicia to the altar, but now it began to look as if she might also have made the better bargain.

"I imagine he's comfortably off," temporised Missy. "I know his generosity to me suggests real wealth, but I suspect it's more that he's a truly generous man. Certainly I shall never, never embarrass him by overspending. However, I do need a few decent clothes – *not* brown! – a couple of winter dresses and a couple of summer ones is all. Oh, Mother, it's so beautiful down in the valley! I don't have any desire to lead a social life, I just want to be alone with my John."

Drusilla looked suddenly troubled. "Missy, there's so little we can give you for a wedding present. But I think, Octavia, that we could spare the Jersey heifer, don't you?"

"We can *certainly* spare the heifer," said Octavia.

"Now that," said Missy, "is what I call a handsome wedding present! We would love the heifer."

"We ought to send her to Percival's bull first," said Octavia. "She's due to come on any time now, so you won't have to wait long for her, and with any luck she'll give you a calf next year too."

Drusilla consulted the clock on the kitchen wall. "If you want to go to Herbert's as well as to Maxwell's, Missy, I suggest we make a start. Then we might be able to fit in a bit of lunch with Julia in her tea room, and tell her the news. My word, she'll be surprised!"

Octavia twitched herself gently, and experienced no pain. "I'm coming too," she announced firmly. "You're not going without me today of all days. If I have to crawl on hands and knees, I'm coming too."

Thus in the late morning Drusilla strolled through the shopping centre with her daughter on one arm, and her sister on the other.

It was Octavia who spied Mrs. Cecil Hurlingford on the opposite side of the road; Mrs. Cecil was the wife of the Reverend Dr. Cecil Hurlingford, Byron's Church of England minister, and everyone went in fear and trembling of her tongue. "Dying of curiosity, aren't you, you old besom?" muttered Octavia through her teeth, smiling and bowing so frostily that Mrs. Cecil thought the better of crossing the road to see what was what with the Missalonghi gaggle.

Then Drusilla completed the routing of Mrs. Cecil by suddenly shouting with laughter and pointing one shaking finger in Mrs. Cecil's direction. "Oh, Octavia, Mrs. Cecil hasn't recognised Missy! I do believe she thinks we've got one of the Caroline Lamb Place women in tow!"

All three of the ladies of Missalonghi dissolved into laughter, and Mrs. Cecil Hurlingford tottered into Julia's tea room to get away from so much unseemly mirth, all apparently directed at *her*.

"What an uproar!" crowed Octavia.

"The bigger the better," said Missy, entering Herbert Hurlingford's clothing emporium.

That whole experience was a terrific tonic, between Uncle Herbert's flabbergasted imitation of a codfish when Missy proceeded to buy men's shirts and trousers for herself, and James's tongue-tied terror when she proceeded to buy lengths of lavender-blue taffeta, apricot silk, amber velvet, and cyclamen wool. Recovering somewhat after Missy left him to go to James, Herbert debated as to whether he should relieve his feelings by ordering the hussy from his premises; then when she paid for her purchases in gold, he changed his mind and humbly rang up the sale. Staggering as Missy's visit was, he really only had half a mind to pay to it and her, for the other half was occupied in wondering what was going on up at the bottling plant, where the extraordinary meeting of shareholders was taking place. The shopkeeping Hurlingfords had despatched Maxwell as their representative, acknowledging that Maxwell had the best and bitterest tongue, and understanding that he would fight as hard for them as for himself. Business must go on as usual, after all, and if the bottling plant and its corollary activities like the baths and the hotel and the spas was going to go west, then the shops became more important than ever to their respective owners.

"You may deliver these to Missalonghi this afternoon, James," said Missy grandly, and slapped a gold sovereign down on the counter. "Here, this is for your trouble. And while you're about it, you can go into Uncle Maxwell's and pick up my grocery order as well. Come, Mother, Aunt Octavia! Let us go to Aunt Julia's for lunch."

The three ladies of Missalonghi swept out of the shop more royally than they had swept in.

"Oh, this is such fun!" chuckled Octavia, whose walk was just about normal. "I have never enjoyed myself so much!"

Missy was enjoying herself too, but less simply. It had been a shock to find the promised thousand pounds had actually been deposited for her, and even more of a shock to be treated with great civility by Quintus Hurlingford, the bank manager; John Smith had instructed him to pay Missy's withdrawals in gold, since the deposit had been in gold. A thousand pounds!

Well, she had her dress materials and her shirts and her trousers, and several pairs of pretty shoes into the bargain. She really didn't need anything else. If she kept a hundred pounds of that amazing thousand, it would be more than enough to last her until her allowance was replenished at this same time next year. After all, when had she ever owned more than a shilling or two? She would therefore use the bulk of her allowance to buy Mother and Aunt Octavia a little pony-and-trap. The pony wouldn't eat the place out the way a bigger horse would, they could manage its harnessing with ease, and never again would they have to walk anywhere, or humble their pride by begging that a conveyance be sent for them. Yes, they should go in style to Alicia's wedding in a smart pony-and-trap!

The hundred pounds Julia had realised from the sale of her shares was already being spent; half the tea room was roped off, and two workmen were toiling at stripping and sanding.

Once she ceased apologising for the mess, Julia gathered her wits together sufficiently to absorb the full splendour of Missy's outfit. "It's a superb dress and hat, dear," she said, "but isn't the colour a little *lairy*?"

"Definitely lairy," admitted Missy, without shame. "But oh, Aunt Julia, I am so sick to death of brown, and can you name a colour further from brown than this? Besides, it suits me, don't you think?"

Yes, but does it suit my tea room? was the question Julia burned to ask, then decided it would be unpardonable to criticise her benefactress. And due to the renovations there weren't many patrons today; she would just have to hope no one would decide she had thrown open her doors to the likes of Caroline Lamb Place. Oh! That must have been what Mrs. Cecil Hurlingford was gobbling about! Oh, dear! Oh, dear dear dear!

In the meantime she had ushered the ladies of Missa-

The Ladies of Missalonghi

longhi to her very best table, and shortly thereafter served them an assortment of sandwiches and cakes, and a big pot of tea.

"I'm going to have a striped paper on the walls in cream and gold and crimson," she said, sitting down to join her guests, "and my chairs will be re-upholstered in a matching but brighter brocade. I'm having the moulding on the ceiling picked out in gilt, canaries in gold cages, and pots of tall palms everywhere. Let Next Door" – her head tilting scornfully towards the wall she shared in common with the Olympus Café – "compete with *that*!"

Drusilla's mouth was open to unburden herself of the news that Missy was married to John Smith and that John Smith was a rich man rather than a jailbird, when Cornelia Hurlingford erupted through the doors and descended upon them, her various scarves and ribbons trailing behind her like moulting feathers from a peacock's tail.

Cornelia and Julia lived together above the Weeping Willow Tea Room, which Julia did not own outright. She paid a large rent to her brother Herbert, who regularly assured her that one day she would have paid enough, between the rent and what her house and five acres had fetched, to buy the premises.

As well as sharing their living arrangements, the two maiden sisters also shared and relished every morsel of information their public occupations garnered, but mostly Cornelia, the less excitable of the two, could wait until

Chez Chapeau Alicia closed its doors for the day; Alicia did not permit her to leave the shop while ever it was open. Obviously whatever she had to impart was urgent enough to run the risk of incurring Alicia's wrath, and so bursting was Cornelia with her news that Missy's scarlet outfit got no more than a cursory glance.

"Guess what?" she gasped, plumping herself down on a chair and forgetting she was supposed to be the formidably elegant and snooty sales dame of a formidably elegant and snooty one-off millinery establishment.

"What?" asked everyone, well aware of these various facts, and therefore prepared to be tremendously impressed.

"Alicia ran off with Billy's chauffeur this morning!"

"*What?*"

"She did, she did! She eloped! At *her* age! Oh, what a circus is going on at Aurelia's! Hysterics and tantrums all over the place! Little Willie nearly tore the house apart looking for Alicia because he refused to believe what her note to him said, and Billy was roaring like a gale because he had to go to some important meeting at the plant when what he really wanted to do was set the police onto his chauffeur! They carted Aurelia off to bed as stiff as a board, and had to send for Uncle Neville when she kept holding her breath until she passed out, and then Uncle Neville gave her such a wallop across the ears because he was cross at being called out for nothing, and he called her no better than a spoiled baby, so that set her off screaming, and she's still screaming! Oh, and Edmund is sitting on a chair just twitching, and Ted and Randolph are trying to pull him together so he can go to the meeting at the plant. But the worst of it is that Alicia and the chauffeur went off in Billy's brand new motorcar, for all the world as if they owned it!"

Cornelia ended her breathless recital with a bellow of laughter, Missy joined her, and one by one the others came in to ring a peal of glorious mirth over the events at Mon Repos. After that catharsis everyone felt absolutely tiptop, and settled to a quieter but no less enjoyable dissection of Missy's marriage and Alicia's elopement, not to mention lunch.

John Smith arrived at Missalonghi just before five o'clock, looking very pleased with himself. He shook his mother-in-law's hand with great affability, but refrained from kissing her, a piece of good sense she heartily approved of. The handshake he also offered Octavia disappointed her, but she had to admit, looking at him properly for the first time, that he was a fine figure of a man. Of course the suit aided her impression, as did the fresh haircut and neatly trimmed beard. Yes, Missy had nothing to be ashamed of in her choice of a life's partner, and to Octavia's way of thinking, his fifteen years of seniority made him just the right age for a husband.

He seemed a nice man on the inside too, for he made himself easily at home in the kitchen and sniffed at the scent of roast lamb appreciatively.

"I hope you and Missy will stay to dinner?" asked Drusilla.

"We'd love to," he said.

"What about the road home? It isn't going to be too risky after dark?"

"Not at all. The horses know it blindfold."

He leaned back in his chair and raised one eyebrow at his wife, who was sitting opposite and just beaming at him with a pride in him his first wife had certainly never owned. What fools men were! They always went after the pretty women, when their intelligence should tell them the homely ones were much better bets. However, she looked all right in that bright red getup, not beautiful, certainly not pretty, but interesting. In fact, she looked like the sort of woman most men would want to get to know because they weren't sure what went on inside. Attractive, bumpy nose and all. And as she sat there sparking with life, it was difficult to believe she could die at any moment. His heart twisted, an odd sensation. Tomorrow, tomorrow! Don't think about it until it happens! You are beginning to dwell on it, and you mustn't! Don't think of her death-sentence as a cosmic revenge on you!

Maybe if he could make her happy enough, it wouldn't happen at all. There were such things as miracles, he had seen one or two in his travels. Getting rid of his first wife undoubtedly fell into the category of a miracle.

"I want to talk to you ladies," he said, dragging his eyes

and his mind away from his present wife.

Three faces turned to him with interest. Drusilla and Octavia ceased fussing at the stove and sat down.

"There was a shareholder's meeting at the Byron Bottle Company today," he said, "and management of the company has changed hands. In fact, it passed into my hands."

"*You?*" squeaked Missy.

"Yes."

"Then you're the mystery buyer?"

"Yes."

"But why? Uncle Billy said the mystery buyer had outlaid the kind of money for shares that no one could ever hope to get back! So why?"

He smiled, not attractively; for the first time since meeting him Missy saw a different John Smith, a powerful and flinty John Smith, a John Smith who might not know the meaning of the word mercy. It didn't frighten her and it didn't take her aback; rather, it pleased her. Here was no defeated refugee from life's insistent pressures, here was no weakling. On the outside he was so delightfully relaxed and easygoing, and there were people who might mistake that for weakness even after they knew him very well, perhaps intimately well. Like his first wife? Yes, she could understand how a wife might come to judge him as less than he actually was, if that wife was a rather stupid, self-centred kind of woman.

But he was answering her, so she paid attention to him.

"I had a bone to pick with the Hurlingfords. Present

company excluded, of course. But by and large, I have found the Hurlingfords so damned smug, so sure that their quasi-noble free-settler English origins put them much higher than people like me who have the rattle of leg-irons on their mother's side and full Jew on their father's. I admit I set out to get the Hurlingfords, and didn't care how much it cost me to do it. Luckily I have enough money to buy out a dozen Byron Bottle Companies without ever feeling the pinch."

"But you don't come from Byron," said Missy, bewildered.

"True. However, my first wife was a Hurlingford."

"Really! What was her name?" asked Drusilla, who was one of the clan experts on Hurlingford genealogy.

"Una."

Fortunately Drusilla and Octavia were far too interested in what John Smith was saying, and John Smith himself was far too interested in saying it, to pay any attention to Missy.

She sat in stony stillness, unable to move the smallest part of her. Una. *Una!*

How could her mother and aunt sit there so unresponsive to that name, when they had met her and entertained her in this very house? Didn't they remember the biscuits, the documents?

"Una?" Drusilla was asking herself. "Let me see now... Yes, she would have to be one of the Marcus Hurlingfords from Sydney, which would make Livilla Hurlingford her first cousin and her closest relative here in Byron. Humph!

I never did meet her, but she died a long time ago, of course. A drowning accident, wasn't it?"

"Yes," said John Smith.

Was that it, then? Was that why she glowed? Was that why every time Missy had needed her, she had been there? Was that why so many small incidents had happened so fortuitously in the library? The novels, all leading up to the one about the girl dying of heart trouble. The shares on the desk. The Power of Attorney forms. Una the conveniently handy Justice of the Peace. The impudence and the gay carelessness, so hugely attractive to one as repressed as Missy had been. The scarlet dress and hat *exactly* as it had flowered in Missy's imagination, and exactly the right size too. The curious significance she had managed to give all her words, so that they sank into Missy like water into parched soil, and germinated richly. Una. Oh, Una! Dear, radiant Una.

"But her married name definitely wasn't Smith," Drusilla was saying. "It was much more unusual, like Cardmom or Terebinth or Gooseflesh. He was a very rich man, as I recollect, which was the only reason the second Sir William approved the match. Yes, I see how they would have insulted you, if you were he."

"I was he, and they did indeed insult me."

"*We*," said Drusilla, reaching out her hand to clasp his, "are delighted to welcome you into this branch of the family, my dear John."

The hard John Smith had gone, for the eyes resting on his

mother-in-law were soft, amused in a gentle way. "Thank you. I've changed my name, of course, and I'd prefer you didn't speak of all this ancient history."

"It will go no further than Missalonghi," said Drusilla, and sighed, assuming he had changed his name to sever all the painful memories. The sordid ramifications Missy knew of from John Smith himself were obviously not a part of Hurlingford history in Byron.

"Poor thing, drowning like that," said Octavia, shaking her head. "It must have hit you hard, John. Still, I'm very glad things have turned out the way they have, the bottling plant and all. And isn't it interesting that you've gone and married another Hurlingford?"

"It was a great help today," said John Smith calmly.

"There are Hurlingfords and Hurlingfords, like any other family," said Drusilla with truth. "Una may not have turned out the right sort of wife for you, so perhaps it's better she died so young. Where Missy – *I* think she will make you happy."

He grinned and reached his arm across the table to take hold of Missy's cold clammy hand. "Yes, I think she will too." He managed to kiss the trembling fingers in spite of their distance from where he sat, then he released the hand and gave all his attention to Drusilla and Octavia.

"Anyway, now I'm in control of the Byron Bottle Company and its auxiliary industries, I want to make some much-needed changes. Naturally I shall sit as chairman of the board of directors and Missy will be my vice-chairman, but I also require eight other directors. Now I need a group of busy, interested individuals who will be as concerned about the town and people of Byron as about the bottling plant itself. Today I received the necessary votes to enable me to restructure the board any way I want, and I want to do something so different that when I announced my intentions, I acquired a few more shares! Sir William, Edmund Marshall, the brothers Maxwell and Herbert Hurlingford, and some dozen others sold out to me when the meeting concluded. Their spleen got the better of their judgement, which only confirms what I've suspected for a very long time – they're fools. The Byron Bottle Company is going to get bigger and better! It's going to become more civic-minded, and it's going to diversify its interests."

He laughed, shrugged. "Well, no point in dwelling on the likes of Sir William Hurlingford, is there! I want *women* on my board, and I want to start with you two ladies and the Misses Julia and Cornelia Hurlingford. All of you have coped magnificently with your hardships, and you certainly don't lack courage. It may be a radical departure to staff a board of directors with women, but in my opinion most boards already consist of women – *old* women."

He lifted that magical eyebrow at Drusilla and Octavia, who were listening to him in spellbound silence. "So? Are you interested in my offer? Naturally you'll be paid directors' fees. The previous board paid each of its members five thousand pounds per annum, though, I warn you, I shall cut that figure to two thousand pounds."

"But we don't know what to do!" cried Octavia.

"Most boards don't, so that's no handicap. The chairman is John Smith, remember, and John Smith will teach you every rope. Each of you will have a specific area to deal with, and I know you'll look at hoary problems with fresh eyes and new problems with the kind of unorthodoxy a usual board can't match."

He looked at Drusilla sternly. "I'm waiting on your answer, Mother. Are you going to join my board, or not?"

Drusilla shut her gaping mouth with an audible snap. "Oh, indeed I am! And so are the others, I'll see to that."

"Good. Then the first item of business you have to deal with is who we're going to appoint to the remaining four board places. Women, mind!"

"I must be dreaming," said Octavia.

"Not at all," said Drusilla, at her most majestic. "This is real, sister. The ladies of Missalonghi have come into their own at last."

"What a day!" sighed Octavia.

What a day, indeed. The last of it was going on outside the open back door, which faced west. So did Missy's chair. She could see the great fanning ribbons of high cloud dyed as scarlet as her dress, and the apple-green sky between them, and the mass of blossom on the fruit trees in the orchard, drifts of white and pink gone pinker in that lovely waning sun. But her mind and her eyes, normally so receptive to the natural beauty of the world, were not preoccupied with that glory. For Una was standing in the doorway, smiling at her. Una. Oh, Una!

"Don't ever tell him, Missy. Let him believe his love and care cured you." Una chuckled gleefully. "He's a darling man, darling, but he has a terrible temper! It's not in your nature to provoke it, but whatever you do, don't tempt fate by telling him about your heart trouble. No man likes to be the dupe of a woman, and he's already had a fair taste of that. So mark what I say – don't ever, ever tell him."

"You're leaving," said Missy desolately.

"With knobs on I'm leaving, darling! I've done what I was sent to do, and now I'm going to take a well-deserved rest on the softest, fattest, pinkest, *champagniest* cloud I can find."

"I can't do it without you, Una!"

"Nonsense, darling, of course you can. Just be good, and especially be good in bed, and you can't go wrong. That is, as long as you heed my warning – *don't ever tell him the truth!*"

That exquisite radiance welling from within Una had fused with the last of the sun; she stood a moment longer in the doorway with the light pouring through her and out of her, then she was gone.

"Missy! Missy! Missy! Are you all right? Are you in pain? Missy! For God's sake, answer me!"

John Smith was standing over her, chafing her hands, a look of desperate horror in his eyes.

She managed to smile up at him. "I'm quite all right, John, truly. It's been the day. Too much happiness!"

"You'd better get used to too much happiness, my little love, because I swear I shall drown you in it," he said, and caught his breath. "You're my second chance, Missalonghi Smith."

A chill breeze puffed in through the open door, and just before Drusilla reached to shut it out, it whispered for Missy's ears alone, "Never tell him! Oh, please, *never* tell him!"